HEARTS IN PERIL

Buried Memories

Mary Alford

Annie's®
AnniesFiction.com

Books in the Hearts in Peril series

Buried Memories
In Too Deep
Christmas Conspiracy

... and more to come!

Buried Memories
Copyright © 2022 Annie's.

All rights reserved. No part of this publication may be reproduced, stored in a retrieval system, or transmitted in any form or by any means—electronic, mechanical, photocopying, recording or otherwise—without the prior written permission of the publisher. The only exception is brief quotations in printed reviews. For information address Annie's, 306 East Parr Road, Berne, Indiana 46711-1138.

The characters and events in this book are fictional, and any resemblance to actual persons or events is coincidental.

Library of Congress-in-Publication Data
Buried Memories / by Mary Alford
p. cm.
I. Title
2022939356

AnniesFiction.com
(800) 282-6643
Hearts In Peril™
Series Creator: Shari Lohner
Series Editor: Amy Woods

10 11 12 13 14 | Printed in China | 9 8 7 6 5 4 3 2 1

1

The storm hit with a flash of lightning that split the sky in front of Eve Cameron's white SUV. A frantic breath later, heavy rain and wind slammed into her with enough force to move the vehicle on the road. Eve clutched the steering wheel in a death grip and struggled to keep the SUV between the ditches. For the past hour, dark clouds had boiled up all around, slowly gathering with nightfall into what had all the makings of a tremendous storm. Almost as if the weather itself were mirroring the turmoil growing inside her.

Let me come with you. Her mother's parting words came back to haunt. As much as Eve wanted to rely on her mother's strength to get through this difficult journey home, Melanie Cameron had her own ugly memories waiting for her at Lourdes Mansion. Ones that had nothing to do with the accident twelve years earlier. Her marriage had crumbled soon after. Her husband, Eve's father, had abandoned them when they needed him the most.

For months following the move to Syracuse, Eve had listened to her mother cry herself to sleep. Eve's father's betrayal still had the power to reduce her strong and confident mother to the broken woman she'd been back then.

Which was why Eve hadn't wanted to burden her mother with the heartbreaking memories returning to the family's estate were bound to stir up. She'd vowed to fight the demons waiting for her there alone. *Brave words*, she told herself. Yet the closer she came to Winter Lake, New York, the more the stress between her shoulder blades seemed to confirm they were just that—words. The urge to turn around and return to her sanctuary in Syracuse was hard not to heed. The storm felt as if the universe were telling her to obey that urge.

Truth be told, Eve had thought about canceling the trip almost from the beginning. She'd picked up the phone a dozen times to call her grandmother. Each time, Gran's sweet face came to mind, and Eve couldn't do it. Jane had asked for help to prepare the estate for sale, and Eve was determined not to let her down no matter how difficult it might be for her personally. As a real estate agent, this was Eve's forte. She'd been happy to follow in the footsteps of her grandfather, who had started a real estate development venture later in life. He'd handed over control of the logging business to his sons, Jacob and Samuel, and followed his dream. Like Eve.

As the heavy torrents continued to bombard the windshield, Eve clicked the wipers up as high as they would go. The blades struggled to keep up with the onslaught. Another blast of wind shoved the SUV closer to the rain-filled ditch. Eve bit back a scream and battled to keep the vehicle on the road.

She let off the gas pedal and slowed her speed as the deluge of water didn't let up. A few more miles until she reached the turnoff to Lourdes Mansion.

Almost there. Almost home.

Home. Nothing about the possibility of reaching her childhood home filled her with anticipation.

Eve couldn't decide which was worse—the storm barreling down on her now, or the shrouded past waiting to pounce at her former family home.

For twelve years she'd known there was something more to the explosion than what she'd been told. Why else would her mind block out what had happened that night? Her best friend had died. Eve had been thrown from the explosion site and injured. She'd suffered minor burns that healed in time, but it was the gaps in her memory that scared her the most. She'd been examined by dozens of doctors. All believed that what she'd seen that night must have been so horrible her brain simply refused to process it.

Eve wiped her damp palms on her jeans one at a time, keeping the other on the wheel. There was nothing to be nervous about. Gran would be there waiting for her with a big smile and a hug. They'd spend hours catching up over a cup of her grandmother's delicious homemade hot chocolate. Everything would be okay.

So why didn't it feel that way?

Though she couldn't see the woods through the rain, the family's property had begun some distance back. Beyond the trees separating the road from the massive stone wall around the property, followed by the manicured grounds of the mansion, lay a wealth of memories. All had been good ones—until that night. Everything changed with the explosion that had claimed Christy's life. While Eve's injuries had eventually healed, the impact of that night had reverberated beyond what she ever could have imagined. It completely destroyed any future Eve might have had with her high school sweetheart, Trent Walsh, and ultimately cost Eve her father's love. It was funny to consider how a simple twist of fate could change one's life so drastically.

Though she hated to worry her mother, with the added stress of the storm, Eve really wanted to hear Melanie's voice. She'd simply check in for a second. Say hello. Find out what her mother was doing. Pretend everything was okay and try to ignore the pit of dread in her stomach.

Using voice command to operate her phone, Eve selected the contact marked *Mom* and waited. Nothing but a busy signal. The storm must have been playing havoc with cell reception. Eve cancelled the call and concentrated on driving while trying to prepare herself emotionally for what lay ahead. She hadn't been back to Lourdes Mansion since the night she'd been carried away in an ambulance. After a week in the hospital, her physical injuries had begun to heal, but the outright terror she'd experienced at the possibility of returning to her family home had increased.

And the biggest blow to her heart had come when Eve's father stopped by the hospital to tell her mother he didn't want to be part of her life or Eve's anymore. He hadn't even bothered to say goodbye to Eve. Her whole world had collapsed. She'd gone into survival mode. Doing what had to be done to heal.

And she was returning to the place where it had all happened. Eve was terrified of what might be revealed if she finally untangled those missing memories.

"Don't think about that now." The words rushed out on a shaky breath. She'd only be there a few days, long enough to take the necessary photos and create a workup of the estate's assets for Gran. The rest of the sales process she could handle from the home she shared with her mother back in Syracuse. Besides, it would be good to see her grandmother again. The last time had been at Grandpa Alfred's funeral the previous winter, and the days had been filled with sadness. Her grandmother had lost the love of her life and Eve, the grandfather she adored, who had been like a father after her own deserted her.

When Gran had first called to discuss the prospect of selling Lourdes Estate, it had broken Eve's heart all over again. The estate had been in the Lourdes family for more than a hundred years. Still, she understood her grandmother's reasons for wanting to sell. The estate sat on almost two hundred acres of pristine woodland. The house itself was almost seven thousand square feet, every inch of it filled with memories of Grandpa Alfred.

Eve tried the phone again with the same result. A shiver sped down her back. She was out here alone without any means of communicating with the outside world. Against her will, the shadowy unknown crowded in. Had she made a terrible mistake by agreeing to return to Lourdes Mansion?

Headlights struck the rearview mirror suddenly, releasing her from the mire of the past. Someone else was on the road. Until that moment, she hadn't seen a single vehicle since she'd left Winter Lake. Somehow, knowing there was another soul out in the weather was comforting.

A clap of thunder made Eve jump nervously, and her heart pounded a frantic cadence in time with the throbbing in her head—all due to the anxiety that had been building since she started the trip.

She leaned forward and tried to see beyond the hood of the vehicle through the sheets of rain.

The lights in the mirror grew brighter. Closer. Was it her imagination, or had the vehicle covered the space between them in the short amount of time her attention had been focused on the road ahead?

She tossed an anxious look over her shoulder. The driver's headlights were on bright, the glare blinding. There was no way the person behind the wheel couldn't see her SUV. Why weren't they slowing down?

Eve picked up her speed to keep from being hit. She edged around a curve in the road and caught a glimpse of the vehicle behind her. It appeared to be a small, dark-colored sedan.

Knives of pain stabbed into her shoulder blades from the strain and being hunched over the steering wheel. At least the driver appeared to have fallen back a little and was no longer on her bumper. She chuckled at herself. Of course there was nothing sinister going on. Merely her frightening past bleeding into the present. The driver probably hadn't realized how close he'd gotten in the downpour.

She leaned forward once more, her full attention on to the rain-slicked road. The turnoff to the estate appeared up ahead on the left. Eve put on her blinker, hoping to warn the driver behind her to slow down. Before she reached the turnoff, the other vehicle suddenly appeared once more, inches off her bumper. Almost as if the driver was purposely trying to intimidate her. The knot in her stomach tightened.

Eve pressed down on the gas and put space between them, searching for a place to get off the road. With the storm not letting up, it was impossible to see anything beyond the headlights. She struggled not to panic when the vehicle mirrored her every move, confirming the horrifying truth. She was being targeted. Tension threatened to swallow her up. Eve was in a life-or-death situation she was ill-equipped to control.

She commanded the phone to call for assistance. Her heart sank when all she heard was that awful busy signal. When she pressed the pedal harder, the SUV spun on the slick road. Eve screamed and fought to get back on track.

With the blinding lights keeping her from seeing anything, the turnoff flashed by in a blur while the danger she faced battered her terrified brain. She was alone with someone trying to force her off the road. Her thoughts ran down all sorts of dark byways. Was it some random attack, or had the driver been waiting for her specifically? But that was impossible, surely. The only people who knew she would be arriving tonight were her grandmother and her mother.

The vehicle slammed into her full force. Momentum flung her body forward. Her neck whiplashed. Through it all, Eve somehow managed to keep her hands on the wheel as the SUV spun sideways and careered toward the ditch.

She fought with everything she had and somehow controlled the momentum. With her heart threatening to explode from her chest, the headlights behind her suddenly disappeared. Eve jerked around in her seat. Nothing but blackness. Where had the car gone?

She had to get off the road as quickly as possible. As soon as she was safe, she'd call the Winter Lake police and report the incident.

The fear was almost paralyzing. Eve slowed enough to make a safe U-turn. Midway through the move the bright headlights flipped back on and the car slammed into her again. She screamed in terror as the car struck her broadside and came within inches of striking her door. The SUV spun on the slippery pavement, the world outside a blur. When the SUV straightened out, she was heading straight off the road. Eve hit the brakes and did her best to stop the trajectory, but it was a losing battle.

"Oh no, oh no, oh no." She wasn't even aware of saying the words. It was as if she were watching the events happen to someone else. The SUV launched itself into the air over the ditch. It slammed into the rough terrain beyond, blowing tires, and plowed through the earth as it sped over downed tree branches and brush.

A dark form appeared straight ahead. Eve blinked rapidly. A tree! She stomped on the brakes without any response, then yanked the wheel hard to the left. Too late. She was all out of options.

The SUV slammed into the tree head-on. The airbags exploded. The force of the sudden stop sent Eve flying forward, and her seat belt caught violently, knocking the air from her lungs. Eve was slung sideways. She struck her head against the door frame and everything went black.

When she came to, her head throbbed mercilessly. She gently touched the spot and brought back blood.

Smoke billowed from the damaged engine. The tires were gone. There would be no driving the SUV out, and the person who attacked her could be waiting for her to leave the vehicle. If being run off the road was a precursor of her attacker's plans for her, she was in real trouble.

Eve hit the locks. She stared anxiously into the heavy darkness broken only by her headlights. The phone wouldn't pick up a signal. She couldn't stay here forever.

Focus. The SUV wouldn't be readily visible from the road, but if her attacker had gone to such lengths to force her off the road, he'd probably be watching where she'd gone and would come after her.

Eve caught sight of headlights close to the place where she'd left the road. The vehicle appeared to be stopping. A car door slammed shut. He was coming. She tried to free the seat belt, but the crash had damaged the clasp. It wouldn't budge. As Eve continued to jab her fingers against the latch, a figure appeared in the pouring rain.

Please, oh, please.

The figure advanced through the woods, making straight for her vehicle. Eve's startled eyes latched onto the person coming her way, while her fingers stilled on the seat belt. He reached for the door handle—rattled it—then knocked on the window. She bit back a scream when his face appeared in the darkness, inches away.

"Are you okay?"

Through the fog of terror in her mind, she recognized the voice.

"If you're hurt, I can help you, but you'll have to unlock the door."

"Trent?" she exclaimed in disbelief. Trent was here. She couldn't believe it. Relief poured through Eve's limbs, leaving them weak. The man standing before her was the very one she hadn't been able to forget no matter how much she told herself there was no future for them. Part of her still loved him. Would always love him.

Her trembling fingers fumbled with the lock and managed to free it. Trent pulled the door open, wearing an expression of shock that matched hers.

"Eve?" His familiar husky voice washed over her. "What are you doing here? What happened? Are you all right?" He kept his attention on her face as if he wasn't sure he could trust what his eyes told him.

As Eve continued to gape at the older version of her high-school sweetheart, she remembered the man who ran her off the road. What if he was still out there? Both she and Trent could be in danger.

Words tumbled from her mouth in a rush. She wasn't sure any of it made sense. The shock on Trent's handsome face proved how unbelievable her story sounded. "He might still be close. I can't get the seat belt free. Help me." Her voice quaked.

"Hang on." Trent leaned over her to work on the latch. Eve sucked in a breath and bit her bottom lip. She hadn't been alone with Trent in years. At Grandpa Alfred's funeral, they'd shared an awkward hug followed by a few superficial words. When she'd ended things between them twelve years earlier, she hadn't really given him an explanation. Eve had simply left, knowing that if she were to survive the accident and her father's abandonment, she had to let go of everything associated with her old life—including Trent.

Eve shrank against the seat when his arm brushed hers, and her reaction to his touch scared her. The scent of his aftershave reminded her of the woods in winter.

The seat belt clasp finally gave way. She was free, yet she couldn't move. Her gaze collided with Trent's deep brown eyes. He pulled in a breath and stepped back.

Eve snapped out of her shock and scrambled from the SUV and straight into his arms. She was safe. As long as he was there, she was safe.

As Trent held her tight, the terrifying reality of her situation crashed over her. Someone had tried to kill her. They'd almost succeeded.

And she had no idea why.

2

Trent stared into the frightened eyes of the woman who would always hold a piece of his heart, unable to believe she was actually there. It had been twelve years. She'd never once returned to the Lourdes family estate. Never explained why she broke his heart. Instead, she'd refused every single one of his calls until he'd finally given up. Nothing he could imagine explained what had brought her back now.

Against his will, their final ugly exchange came to mind, the hurt bubbling up to the surface. For most of his life, he'd loved her. Trent had planned to ask her to be his wife the summer of the accident. At least a dozen times he'd carried the ring in his pocket, waiting for the perfect moment to propose. The right spot. She deserved the best.

But that moment had never come.

When she'd told him it was over between them and she was leaving Winter Lake for good, Trent had felt as if he'd been hit by a train.

"We have to get out of here, Trent. Now. We're in danger." Eve's panicked words pulled him away from painful memories best left alone. She peered into the rain-soaked darkness as if expecting someone to emerge. "He might still be out there."

Trent looked over his shoulder while a prickle of unease made its way down his spine. Truth be told, it had followed him the entire trip from his office in Winter Lake. All because of the one case he couldn't let go. Maybe it was because of the final victim and his promise to her family, or the little things that had happened recently which he couldn't explain, but a sense of being followed had been prevalent in his mind lately. Almost as if the hunter had become the hunted.

"I tried everything, but I couldn't keep the SUV on the road." Her nervous gaze found him again. What she'd said scared the daylights out of him. She'd been run off the road—exactly like the other victims in his last case. Had Eve fallen into a killer's crosshairs? "Trent, he deliberately ran me off the road." She shuddered.

Her words sent a different kind of terror through him. The Roadside Stalker's MO was to run his victims off the road before abducting them.

Trent focused on the driver's side of her SUV. A large concave area started just behind the door and ran to the rear of the vehicle. If the driver had hit any further forward, Eve might not have survived.

Deliberately. That one word stuck in his mind. Had his continual digging into the case brought the killer out of hiding? "Tell me everything." There was a sharpness to his tone that had nothing to do with her.

He'd had no idea she was coming back to Lourdes Estate.

If the explosion wasn't an accident, then Eve could be in danger.

Her grandfather's warning to Trent left him with a sense of dread, as it had that first time Alfred had told him to watch out for Eve. Three months had passed since Alfred's death, and he still didn't fully understand what the older man had been trying to tell him.

But neither Alfred nor Trent had expected the danger to come from Trent's past rather than Eve's.

He'd thought Eve was safe at the home she shared with her mother miles away. Jane hadn't said differently. Yet here Eve was, and he had no idea where the threat was coming from.

"He must have followed me," Eve was saying. Trent shoved his fears aside and focused on her words. "I noticed the car behind me right before I reached the cutoff. At first, I thought it was simply someone else caught in the storm." She told him about the frightening experience of being struck that first time. The driver had tried to fool her by switching off his lights and then flipping them back on to freeze her before that final blow that sent her off the road.

Trent's jaw tightened when he thought of someone wanting to hurt her. "Who else knew you were coming here tonight?"

"No one except for Gran and my mother."

It was on the tip of his tongue to ask why she'd come back after so many years, but she was soaking wet and shivering from the cold rain.

"Let's get you out of the weather. My SUV's back up on the road." He crooked a thumb in that direction before placing his arm around her shoulders in a protective gesture that came as naturally as his next breath.

She leaned into him, driving home how rattled she truly was by the incident. Otherwise, she'd never lean on him. They picked their way through the drenched woods as quickly as they dared. He needed to get her to a safe place and out of the open. While they walked, he scanned the woods around them and tried to rein in his turbulent thoughts, yet one thing refused to go away. She'd been forced off the road. That couldn't be a coincidence. It was the Roadside Stalker's MO for disabling his victims.

The final case he'd worked as a detective for the Winter Lake police department—the Roadside Stalker—was the one he hadn't been able to solve, and ultimately responsible for his leaving the force. The Stalker's last victim came to mind. Samantha Hart. Her car had been struck in much the same manner as Eve's, like the six other victims who had perished before her. The Stalker had taken Samantha before help could arrive. Trent and his partner, Detective Luke Carter, had found Samantha days later, clinging to life. She'd died on the way to the hospital. If he'd been just a few minutes earlier . . .

Even though he was no longer on the force, every spare minute he'd had for the past two years had been dedicated to working Samantha's case. As a private investigator, he had more freedom to pursue leads that hadn't panned out previously. Mainly that the killer must have a connection to the area. Perhaps he'd lived here at one time or still had family around.

For several weeks, Trent had believed he might be getting closer to finding out the killer's identity. He'd noticed a strange car following him. Had seen it parked near the road to the Lourdes. The license plate had been removed, and every time Trent tried to get close, the driver sped away. Had the Stalker returned to Winter Lake to continue his macabre game, or had he been here all along?

The thought of Eve in the sights of such a cold-blooded killer chilled his blood.

He tugged her closer as they trudged through the soaked underbrush and traversed the ditch filling with water. Trent opened the passenger door to his SUV and helped Eve climb into its warmth. The goosebumps working their way up his arms had nothing to do with the chill. He carefully scanned the countryside. Where had the attacker gone? Trent hadn't heard another vehicle leaving when he'd arrived. But did that mean the driver was in hiding, or had he sped away right after sending Eve's SUV off the road?

Trent flipped up the collar of his jacket and hurried around to the driver's side as the rain continued to bombard. The predicted storm had hit with a fury that hadn't been forecasted. He wondered how long the road to the Lourdes family estate would remain open. If the river flooded its banks, it could take out the bridge, and there'd be no getting in or out. The thought didn't sit well.

He cranked up the heater to take away the chill of the night. Once it blasted against the water on his face, he turned to Eve, grateful to see her shivering had subsided. Her strained expression reminded him of the night of the explosion that had killed her good friend, Christy Templeton, and sent Eve to the hospital. When he heard the news, he'd rushed to see her. Trent had been so certain she wouldn't recover from her injuries, so sure he'd lose her forever.

And he had. At the time, he had no idea he would lose her in a way he never could have imagined.

Trent swallowed deeply. *Let it go.* "When did you first notice the car?" he asked, trying to focus on the problem at hand.

Her voice was tight as she relived the nightmare. "I was almost to the turnoff to the estate. He drove up until he was right on my bumper. I thought maybe the driver didn't see me—until he struck my vehicle." She pulled in a breath and fixed her gaze on him. "This was no accident, Trent. That driver attacked me. The only question is why?"

He couldn't stop himself from comparing the similarities to Samantha and the other victims. "Did you get a good look at the car? Can you describe it? The driver?"

She shook her head. "No, not the driver, but I did see the car. It was a small sedan. Maybe black or dark blue."

The pit in his stomach tightened uncomfortably. That matched the description of the car that had been following him. "I'm calling this in. If this attack was intentional, your vehicle has now become a crime scene."

Eve's eyes widened at what he'd said. While he dialed his former partner, Trent's mind raced in all kinds of uncomfortable directions. He waited through two rings before Luke picked up.

"It's me. I'm here with Eve Cameron." Trent did his best to explain what had happened and gave Luke their current location. "We need help right away. I don't see the car, but there's a good chance the driver may still be around."

"Are you safe?" The urgency in Luke's tone was not wasted on Trent.

He peered into the soggy darkness. "I think so. We're in my SUV. To be safe, we'll pull back closer to the Lourdes estate entrance and away from the immediate scene. There's been no sign of the vehicle or the driver since I've been here. Still..." He didn't finish. As a former detective, he understood that the man who had come after Eve so aggressively wouldn't necessarily give up easily. There was a good chance he was still out there. Watching. Waiting for the right moment.

"Copy that. We're on our way. Stay safe, brother." Luke ended the call.

Trent glanced briefly at Eve before making a U-turn on the road. He drove back to the estate entrance and parked facing the road. Once they'd stopped, he retrieved his handgun from underneath the driver's seat. Eve's eyes widened at the sight of it. "It's merely a precaution," he said to reassure her.

Her full attention remained on the weapon. "I thought you got out of law enforcement."

Trent wasn't surprised that she knew about his life. She and Alfred had been close up until his death. Alfred had told Trent about his weekly calls with his granddaughter. He'd given detailed accounts of her life in Syracuse. Trent believed Alfred had always held out hope that he and Eve would find their way back to each other someday. Trent didn't have the heart to tell him that he still had no idea why Eve had chosen to end their relationship.

"Yes, but I still carry a weapon for my line of work."

Her frown deepened as she focused on him. "Grandpa Alfred told me you had opened your own private investigative agency." She shook her head. "I guess I never really thought you'd have a need for a gun."

How could he tell her the one case that haunted him daily was one of the main reasons he kept a weapon with him at all times?

"It's necessary," he murmured by way of explanation, even as he wondered if Eve's attacker may have been scared off by his appearance. His cop's instinct stopped him. The idea wouldn't help anything.

"Are you warm enough?" he asked, stuffing his doubts down deep for the moment. Eve had always been good at reading him. She was shaken up enough. He didn't want her picking up on his fears.

"I'm fine." Her weary tone said otherwise. She pinched the spot between her brows.

He'd seen that look many times while working as a detective for the Winter Lake police department. Victims and their families came to him at their worst possible moments.

"What were you doing this far out anyway?" she asked, watching closely for his reaction.

Trent had wondered how long it would take her to ask him this. She'd know he lived and worked in town. As much as he wanted to tell her the truth, Alfred had sworn him to secrecy when he'd come to Trent's office a few weeks before his death and asked Trent to discreetly investigate the events from twelve years before, on the night of the accident.

To say Trent had been surprised was an understatement. To his knowledge, the explosion had been a tragic mishap. But Alfred believed otherwise and was certain the information he'd uncovered might provide a clue about something far more deadly.

"Trent?" He jerked toward the sound of Eve's voice. Before he had the chance to tell her he'd been staying at her family's estate for three months, Trent spotted something alarming. From their vantage point, he could just see the place where Eve's vehicle rested. They'd left headlights on, but there was another light bouncing around the space near the SUV. A flashlight. He'd been right to think the perp hadn't left the area.

Eve leaned forward and gasped when she saw what he did. "He's searching for me."

With the weapon in his hand, Trent shut off the interior light and opened the door. He couldn't let the person get away, but leaving Eve alone could put her in jeopardy if the attacker circled back.

"I have to go after him, Eve, and I can't leave you alone."

Her distressed blue eyes latched onto his as she guessed what he was thinking.

"It'll be okay," he said, anticipating her doubt. "Stay close to me."

He paused with his hand on the door. She probably still remembered him as that teenage boy who took too many risks and got into trouble, but exploring potentially dangerous situations was what he was trained to do. The past swirled around him. So many good times they'd spent together. Lazy summer days spent down at the river on the family's property, swimming and sneaking kisses. Their prom. All the special moments he thought would never end.

Until they had.

With a whole lot of difficulty, Trent forced the past back to where it belonged. In the end, it was because *she* hadn't fought for them that he had been able to let her go.

Trent got out and closed the door as quietly as possible to avoid alerting the perp. He went around to Eve's side and held out his hand. All of her fears were there for him to see as she stepped from the SUV and glued herself to his side.

Adrenaline made him feel as if he moved in slow motion. The rapid beat of his heart created a cadence that was almost loud enough to drown out the sound of his breathing. Trent stopped long enough to get a bead on the perp's location.

With her hand tucked in his, he and Eve crossed the road and stepped off the pavement. The light still hadn't disappeared. The woods enveloped him along with a thick fog that brushed against his skin like a ghostly touch.

The gun in his hand provided a small amount of comfort. He knew how to use it and wouldn't hesitate if needed. Trent could count on one hand the times he'd had to fire his weapon during his time on the force. But it was that last time that stood out in his mind. He'd been close enough to fire at the killer that night before he'd gotten away.

If Eve's roadway aggressor was the same person as Samantha's killer—the Roadside Stalker—was Eve's case simply a random attack? In the past, the killer had stalked his victims for weeks and left a note in their mailboxes before abducting them. There was a possibility the attack wasn't meant for Eve at all. Perhaps, in the rain, he'd mistaken Eve's smaller SUV for Trent's. After all, both vehicles were white, and about the same size. Plus, since he was staying at Lourdes Mansion, it made sense for his vehicle to be on the road to the estate.

Eve's accelerated breathing matched his as they eased toward where the flashlight beam bounced around near her vehicle. The rain had stopped for the time being. The clouds had broken up and a full moon shone down through the trees.

A downed branch cracked under his weight, and the noise echoed all around. He pulled Eve behind the nearest tree a split second before the perp whipped the light in the direction of the sound. It flashed on either side of their hiding spot. Trent held Eve close while they waited and prayed he hadn't scared off the attacker.

Luke had to be close. Trent listened but didn't hear the sirens yet, which might prove a good thing if he could surprise and subdue the perp.

The beam eventually moved away, and Eve expelled a breath. Trent kept her close and peeked around the tree.

"Stay behind me," he whispered close to her ear.

She nodded and waited for him to make a move.

Trent pulled in a breath and stepped out from their cover. With Eve inches behind him, he crept toward the light as fast as he dared. When he'd almost reached it, it vanished. A heavy fog had gathered in the woods and the sole light came from the headlights and the moon filtering through the leaves. His next breath hung in his throat.

Eve ran into his back. "Sorry," she whispered.

Beyond the pounding of his heartbeat, nothing moved. Still, the hairs at the back of his neck wouldn't let him believe the perp had left.

As they continued toward Eve's wrecked SUV, the bright headlights cast a halo of light around the vehicle. Cold soaked through his jacket and clothes down to muscle and bone. At the vehicle, Trent pulled out his phone to use the flashlight app and briefly held it close to the ground. The wet earth was covered in footprints. Some were his and Eve's. Another set led to the front of the vehicle.

"Go to the back of the SUV and get down," he told Eve, then waited while she rushed to the back. Once she was out of sight, he slowly eased forward using the phone to follow the footprints. The hood of the vehicle was still warm. He could almost hear Luke warning him to return to the SUV and wait for backup.

But if it was the Stalker, he couldn't let them get away. Lives were at stake. And he'd promised Samantha. Her family. Himself.

Trent caught a glimpse of movement to the left out of the corner of his eye. He whipped toward it. From the glow of the headlights, a man around Trent's height and build, dressed in dark clothes and a ski mask, charged toward him. The man waved something large above his head.

Before Trent could get off a single shot, something heavy slammed against his head and piercing pain burst from the contact spot. The blow dropped Trent to his knees. His vision blurred. The weapon fell from his hand while he hung onto consciousness by a thread.

Trent squeezed his eyes shut several times to clear his vision. Fuzzy glimpses of a figure retreating through the trees reached past the muddle in his head. His attacker was heading in the direction Trent had come.

Straight for where Eve was hiding.

"No." He wasn't sure if he said the word aloud, but it was enough to get him moving. He stumbled to his feet, the sharp pain in his head making his stomach roil. Somehow, Trent kept his legs under him. Using the phone, he searched around until he found the gun. All he could think about was Eve. He had to keep her safe.

"Please let her be okay." The frantic prayer had barely cleared his lips when a figure emerged through the fog heading for him. He aimed the weapon, thinking the perp had come back to finish him off.

Eve stopped in her tracks when she spotted his gun. "Trent, it's me."

He immediately lowered it. "Sorry, I thought you were him."

She closed the space between them. "Trent, you're hurt," she exclaimed when she spotted the bloody place where he'd been struck.

"It's nothing. I'm okay," he lied. Every second they were out here in the open, both he and Eve were in danger. "We need to get back to the road right away."

He grabbed her hand and started through the woods as fast as physically possible, ignoring the soggy tree branches slapping his face and hands. Soon, the woods thinned. Once they reached the road, Trent rotated in place, his eyes peeled for the man who seemed to have disappeared into thin air.

Keeping his feet beneath him was difficult, but it was critical they reach the SUV and get out of sight. Trent kept a careful eye on their surroundings as they covered the distance.

"What happened back there?" Eve asked once they were safely inside.

Trent secured the locks and laid the handgun on his leg. Having it close made him feel safer. "He came out of nowhere."

Eve chewed her bottom lip as Trent told her about the attack. "He could have killed you. We need to get you to a doctor."

He shook his head and regretted the movement when a throbbing pain made him clutch his temples. "I'll be okay," he murmured as he waited for his vision to clear. "Did you manage to see where he went?"

She shook her head. "No, I didn't see anyone." She rubbed her forehead nervously. "Why is he doing this?"

How could he tell her that he suspected a serial killer from his past was responsible for the horrors she'd experienced that evening?

"I'm not sure," he said instead, because he had no proof and the attack on him didn't fit the killer's profile. Trent scanned the space beyond her shoulder. It was as if the perp had disappeared into the night, as the Stalker had after every single murder.

In the distance, red and blue lights flashed in the countryside, shattering the darkness. Sirens screamed through the night. Luke had brought plenty of backup. A small sense of relief uncoiled some of the tension between Trent's shoulders. *Thank you, God.*

"That's Luke. He'll want to get both our statements," he told Eve, who gave a deep sigh.

Trent watched the lights approaching and recalled something Eve's grandfather had told him in the days before his death.

She could hold the identity of a killer in her blocked memories. If that's the case, he'll come after her eventually.

After tonight, Alfred's words of warning hit home with deadly urgency. Alfred had been right to worry about Eve. But had he been wrong about where the danger would come from?

3

With the attack on Trent dominating her thoughts, Eve had completely forgotten that Trent never answered her question as to why he'd been driving so far out of town. He had a house in town. His work was there. Was he heading to the estate for some reason? He wouldn't have known she was coming home unless Gran told him. She had a feeling he hadn't simply happened to be on that road.

She shifted in her seat once more. "You never told me why you were out this direction, especially in a storm."

Gran kept Eve and her mother updated on what went on around the estate and Winter Lake. When she'd called to ask for Eve's help selling the family estate, she'd mentioned Trent was doing some work around the place, but Eve hadn't pressed for details. Talking about Trent was always awkward.

His intense brown eyes pinned her in place, reminding Eve of all the things she'd once longed for.

"I'm staying at the estate—I have been since your grandfather hired me to find out who's been illegally trapping on the property. I assumed you knew," he added, to her surprise.

A dozen different questions came to mind. The trapping explanation seemed flimsy at best. Still, she wasn't really surprised that Trent would continue to work for her grandfather even after the older man had succumbed to a heart attack. He'd loved Grandpa Alfred almost as much as she had. And that was just who Trent was. He had a hero's heart that wouldn't let him give up on those he loved.

Unlike her.

Guilt threatened to rip her heart to shreds. How different would things have been if she'd had the courage to fight her fear and stand up for their relationship?

Eve swallowed several times and ordered herself not to cry. More than ever, she wished that she could go back in time and redo the events of that night that had destroyed so much. If only she'd fixed the flat on her car, had Christy spend the night, or done any of a dozen little things that would have changed the course of history. If she had, Christy might still be alive. She and Trent might be married with a house full of kids.

She pressed her lips together. The past couldn't be rewritten. Her life was no longer at Lourdes Estate.

Something off the left of the windshield grabbed her attention. Her brain tried to make sense of what she was seeing but couldn't. A loud crack resounded around the countryside, drowning out the sirens heading their way. The driver's side window glass shattered on impact. A bullet whizzed inches past Trent's head and struck the padded dashboard.

"Get down!" he yelled, but all Eve could do was stare in horror at the destroyed window. Trent grabbed her shoulders and pushed her down, covering her body with his. Another crack of gunfire followed.

Eve's heart hammered in time with each shot while she wondered if help would come too late to save them.

The police sirens created an eerie backdrop to the rapid gunshots.

It seemed like forever before it stopped.

"Is it over?" She hadn't realized she'd grabbed hold of Trent's hand and was squeezing it tight.

"Hang on. Stay where you are for now." He stroked her hand with his thumb, and his touch helped her feel safe. He peered outside, searching for the origin of the gunshots. "I don't see anything. You can sit up now."

Eve released his hand and eased to a sitting position. She couldn't stop shaking. In the space of an hour, her fears about returning to Lourdes Mansion had been obliterated by the horrifying events on the way to the estate.

After being pushed off the road and with the night of the explosion foremost in her thoughts, Eve had to wonder if someone was trying to warn her not to come back to the estate. What dark secrets were waiting for her there that would make someone wish to threaten her life?

Eve glanced around at the mayhem that had taken place in a few short minutes. Trent's window had shattered. Glass shards were scattered everywhere in his hair, his clothing, on the seat between them.

"Your face," she whispered.

Trent's forehead, cheeks, and hands were cut and bleeding from the broken glass. Damp cold air blew through the gaping hole in the window. Bullets were lodged everywhere, several far too close to where she and Trent had been.

Shockwaves rippled through her body. Her ears still rang from the gunshots, and her hands trembled uncontrollably. She clasped them together in her lap to keep Trent from noticing.

"Someone tried to kill us." Her brain wouldn't compute what she'd been through.

Trent placed his hands over hers. He didn't deny it.

She'd wanted him to.

"Why?" The word tore from her lips. "Why would someone do this?"

There was something in the look he gave her. "I don't know, but we'll figure it out, Eve. I promise we'll figure it out."

The sirens grew closer. Having Trent with her and knowing the police were nearby gave a small amount of comfort.

"This is so scary." It was a tremendous understatement, but it was all she could come up with at the moment.

Trent remained silent.

Eve couldn't explain it, but she got the sense that he wasn't completely surprised by the evening's events. "Has something like this happened before?"

The fact that he couldn't meet her eye scared her.

"Trent?" she pressed.

Before he could get a single word out, four police vehicles screeched to a halt near the SUV.

"There's Luke. We'll talk about this later," he said. "Why don't you stay here where it's warm? I'll be back soon."

Despite the warm air on her face, the chill that had begun when the car had slammed into her wouldn't go away. She grabbed his arm. "Trent, please tell me."

He slumped back against the seat and shook his head. "It could be nothing."

"But?"

"A few years back there was a serial killer working the county." He waited for her to say something.

Eve remembered Grandpa Alfred mentioning the crimes. She'd been shocked to hear about something so horrible in such a peaceful community. Seven victims, all women between the ages of twenty-five and thirty-five. All had been taken from their cars along a deserted stretch of road, exactly like this one.

"You're talking about the Roadside Stalker." It wasn't a question.

"That's right. Luke and I worked on the case together. We never caught the killer. Damage to each victim's car seemed to indicate that he had crashed into them in order to disable their vehicles prior to the kidnappings."

Reality washed over her. Had she been targeted by a serial killer? Suddenly, she regretted asking.

"But that's where the MO ends, Eve," he told her. "The Roadside Stalker never used a gun. He killed his victims with a knife. He left a note before the attack, and each victim had reported to a friend or family member that they believed someone had been following them. This is different, Eve. Okay?"

She expelled a ragged breath. "Okay."

"Good." His face relaxed with his smile. "We'll figure this out, I promise. I'm not going to let anything happen to you, Eve." He glanced past her to where Luke waited. "You're shivering. Stay here where it's warm. I'll speak to Luke. Try not to worry. We'll get to the bottom of this."

Eve couldn't let go of the similarities between the evening's events and the case Trent had worked, yet part of her wondered—was the attack somehow related to what was locked away in her hidden past? Or did she have a whole other nightmare to worry about?

4

Trent didn't even want to consider that this might be the Stalker. He got out and tried to gather himself before facing Luke.

Alfred had hinted that the explosion twelve years earlier hadn't been an accident at all, and it was possible his terrifying concerns were valid. After discovering some hidden documents, Alfred was positive the explosion had been intentionally set to cover the crime. And he was convinced it had been meant for Eve's father, Henry Cameron. Alfred feared his granddaughter might be in danger because he was certain she had inadvertently seen the face of the person who'd caused the explosion.

"Everyone okay?" Luke materialized beside him and Trent started. "Sorry, brother. Seems you've had quite a night." He pointed to the superficial cuts on Trent's face, and the knot forming on his head from his run-in with the perp.

"You could say that," Trent replied. "Whoever ran Eve off the road obviously meant to finish the job." He indicated the window and explained about the light he and Eve had seen near her disabled vehicle and the attack that had taken place, followed by the shooting.

Luke's expression was grave as he opened the door and spoke to Eve. "It's nice to see you again, Eve. I'm sorry it's under these circumstances." There was a hint of resentment in Luke's tone. The three of them had once been close, along with Christy. Before the explosion, they'd done everything together. After he'd gotten over the shock of Christy's death, Luke was the one who had taken Trent to the hospital to be with Eve.

He'd stayed at Trent's side through the waiting.

When Eve had ended things, Trent had fallen apart—thought his world was over—yet Luke saw him through it, helped him pick up the pieces of his life. They'd joined the police force together and had risen up through the ranks to be detectives. It had always been Luke by his side until Trent left the force. And even then, Luke remained a permanent fixture in his life.

Luke motioned over two patrol officers. "Chances are he took off when he heard our sirens, but I'd like you to check down the road to be sure."

Both officers confirmed the order and returned to their vehicles.

"My guess is he was stationed over there"—Trent pointed to the woods just this side of the Lourdes property wall—"when he started firing. Hopefully, you'll find some shell casings or something."

"Secure the site and any evidence you find until CSI arrives," Luke said to several officers, who headed toward the crime scene. He faced Eve. "Any reason why someone would want to harm you?"

She flinched. "Until tonight I would have said no. Now, I'm not sure."

"If this is our guy, this is definitely a new twist." Luke's concern seemed to double. He, too, knew their killer's MO by heart. "Let's head to your SUV. Once the EMTs have examined you both, you can head home. Have you been having problems with anyone before, maybe something that didn't seem significant at the time like someone following you, or seeing the same person at different places you went?"

Eve shook her head. "No one. I live a very simple life in Syracuse with my mother. I can't imagine why someone would want to hurt me. Do you think this could have something to do with the explosion that took place on my family property when Christy died?"

"What makes you think that?" Luke asked.

Her forehead furrowed as if she were trying to remember something. "I'm not sure. I've always dreaded coming back here because it feels as if there's something waiting for me from that night. Something I'm not sure I want to know."

Her words mirrored Alfred's fears.

Luke kept his expression neutral. "Let's not go there yet. Right now, what we have is a bunch of questions without answers."

Eve slowly nodded. "You're right."

Trent clasped her hand as she climbed from the vehicle. When he would have let go, Eve held his hand tighter.

Natural trauma response, he told himself. It didn't mean anything. And yet the simple gesture reminded him of all the times they'd held hands years ago, when he thought they had the rest of their lives to be together.

He wished the young man he'd been back then had known how fragile their future would be. He wouldn't have taken a moment for granted. He'd have asked her to marry him sooner and whisked her away from the danger that waited to swallow her up.

Trent hadn't realized he'd stopped walking until Eve looked back at him.

"What's wrong?" she asked.

He couldn't change what had already happened. There was the present moment and the future. It was best not to get stuck in the past.

"Nothing."

With her hand tucked in his, they crossed the road. The headlights from Eve's SUV still illuminated the woods, though not as brightly as before.

Luke's flashlight beam picked up the skid marks where Eve's vehicle had left the road. The outcome could have been so much worse. He held her hand a little tighter.

"There's another set of tire tracks heading away." Luke shined the light down the road. "I'm guessing he sped away after he ran you off the road. But if he left then, he must have parked somewhere to go back into the woods later and attack you, Trent."

"You think it's possible he's still around?" Trent asked.

"Don't know." Luke hit the radio. "I need some more help over here. There's a chance the perp might still be in the area."

One of his officers responded to the call. "10-4, Detective. We'll be right there."

When a group of officers reached them, Luke told them to spread out and search the woods. "Let's see if we can get your things," he told Eve before glancing at Trent. "How are you holding up? That's some knot you have there. Not to mention the lacerations."

The headache that continued to grow stronger reminded him of how close he'd come to catching the perp. And how it had almost cost him dearly.

"Just a few surface cuts and a bump," he said, "but I'd like to have them see to Eve. She hit her head pretty hard."

"They'll check you both out." The steel in Luke's tone assured Trent the statement wasn't open for discussion.

Following Luke's lead, Trent kept a careful eye on their surroundings. The attack had taken him by surprise, but the shooting spree went beyond anything he'd witnessed with the killer he and Luke had been chasing.

When they reached the ditch, it was overflowing. Water rushed through at a rapid rate. Trent jumped across it and held out his hand to Eve.

She strained to clasp his hand before jumping. As she landed on the bank next to him, Eve's foot slipped on the muddy ground.

Trent caught her waist and pulled her up beside him.

For a second, she held him tight. Everything about her being in his arms was familiar, right.

She pulled free and he let her go.

They were all soaked to the bone. Even though it was springtime, the damp chill set in deep.

"Let's keep going," Luke said in the awkward silence that followed.

They started walking again. Eve stumbled over a fallen tree branch and Trent reached out to steady her. Her gaze skimmed over his face. Whenever he looked at her, he saw the young girl he'd fallen in love with, the one who'd broken his heart when she told him it was over.

She took a step back and his hands fell away.

At the very least, they were chasing someone who wanted to harm Eve. At the most, a serial killer. The past, his feelings—they didn't matter.

Eve shoved her wet hair from her face. "I'm okay," she murmured.

Trent tightened his jaw and kept moving.

They approached Eve's SUV once more. The driver's side door stood open. It had been closed before.

"Did you leave this door open?" Luke asked.

Eve shook her head, eyes wide.

Luke hit his radio. "Dispatch, how far out is the crime scene unit?"

"They should be rolling up now," Gladys Cartwright, the department's late-shift dispatcher, confirmed.

"Roger, Gladys." Luke ended the transmission. "Until crime scene has had the chance to test for prints, we can't move anything. I'm sorry for the inconvenience," he told Eve. "I'll get your things back to you as soon as possible."

"My bag," Eve said, pointing. "I left it on the passenger seat after I hit the tree." It lay on the passenger floorboard, its contents scattered around.

"He went through it," Trent said. If this was the Stalker, it was possible he had wanted something to take as a memento. With the other victims, he'd taken their driver's licenses.

As if reading his mind, Luke took out latex gloves and flipped through the strewn contents. "License is here," he said, showing it to Trent. "CSI will need to see if they can lift any prints. Ah, there they are." Luke straightened up. "It could be hours before we're done here. Let's get you both back to the road and examined."

Members of the police department's crime scene investigation team descended on the SUV.

After he'd had a word with the team, Luke escorted Trent and Eve to the road where an ambulance had arrived on the scene.

The paramedic in charge treated Trent's cuts and examined his head injury, warning him to be cautious of a possible concussion. Once he was bandaged, Trent stepped away with Luke so the paramedic could treat Eve.

"You know what I'm thinking," Trent told his friend.

"I do." The grim expression on Luke's face proved it hadn't taken him long to come to the same conclusion as Trent. He watched as the paramedic treated Eve. "But there's no note. Her driver's license was still there. And the Stalker never used a gun. It was always a knife."

Trent blew out a sigh. "Yeah, I know. That's throwing me as well. Maybe I interrupted the perp before he could take Eve's driver's license. We can't dismiss this being the work of the Stalker, Luke. It has been two years since he's killed. Maybe he's changing up his MO. He could have continued his killing spree somewhere else."

"I would have noticed," Luke reminded him. He had kept a careful eye out for any murders around the country matching their killer.

"Good point. It could also be connected to Alfred's concerns about Eve's safety," Trent suggested.

Luke wore the same hollow expression Trent recognized from their time chasing the Stalker. "Until we know for certain what's going on, we can't afford to rule out anything. I know Alfred was worried about Eve, but there's been no proof anyone was after her in the past. And if this is connected to the Stalker, it's been two years since he murdered his last victim. Where's he been during that time? Why stop and start back up again?"

Trent had wondered the same. "He could have been living in another part of the country due to work or for some other reason."

"Okay, but why Eve?" Luke asked. "She hasn't lived in Winter Lake in years, long before the killings began. If he's come back to hunt his old grounds, why not choose someone who lives here, like before?"

Trent couldn't answer that question.

"Whatever we're dealing with, I'm glad you're staying at the estate to keep an eye out for Eve. I'm assuming she doesn't know the real reason." Luke raised his eyebrows in question.

"No. Alfred was very clear. Until I found out the truth, he didn't want me to tell the family, not even his wife."

"For now, let's keep it that way. However, at some point, I think you'll have to loop in Eve," Luke said. "I take it you're still working on Samantha's case?"

Trent held up a hand. "I know what you're going to say, and I know the police are also still investigating, but this one's personal to me, Luke. I promised Samantha's parents I'd catch the guy who killed her and I don't intend to let them down."

Luke knew all the reasons, as well as the guilt Trent carried over his failure to save Samantha. "It wasn't your fault, my friend," Luke reminded him, as he had continually for two years.

Still, it didn't help to know Trent had been mere minutes away from reaching Samantha in time to save her.

The note he'd received at his office a few days earlier came to mind. It wasn't postmarked. The note consisted of four words. *Leave the past alone.* The letters had been cut out from magazines like the rest of the Stalker's notes. Trent had handed the note over to Luke. There'd been no fingerprints or any other evidence on the envelope or the note itself.

"If that note was from the killer—and we can't rule out the possibility—then he's back," Luke said quietly.

"Exactly. Do you think the killer came after Eve because of me?" Trent asked.

"I'm not saying that, but I want you to watch your back. And hers. Take Eve home. She looks exhausted." Luke nodded toward the ambulance where the paramedic had finished examining her. "You do too. You've both been through the ringer tonight. Get some rest. I'll call you the minute we have anything."

Trent clapped his hand on Luke's shoulder. "Thank you, brother."

"You're welcome."

Trent headed over to Eve and realized Luke was right. She must be ready to drop.

"How are you feeling?" he asked her.

She waved off his concern. "I'm fine. It's a little bump."

Trent nodded and glanced around at the police activity taking place. "Are you ready to go?"

In a blink of an eye, her demeanor changed. She hugged her arms tight in a defensive gesture that seemed to indicate coming back to Lourdes Mansion hadn't been her idea.

She gathered herself. "I'm sure my grandmother will be anxious. She expected me over an hour ago."

"Do you want to call her?" he asked as they headed for his SUV.

"No. I just want to go home."

He studied her pretty face for a long moment. Why did he get the feeling she wasn't referring to Lourdes Mansion as "home"?

They climbed in, and he started the engine. The heater blasted warm air throughout the space. He could feel it seeping through his chilled limbs, relaxing his muscles.

In the past, when he'd envisioned her homecoming, he'd never imagined it under such traumatic circumstances.

"Thank you." Her whispered words worked their way through his deluge of emotions.

"For what?" He studied her face. She would always be that beautiful woman he'd fallen in love with, but time—and perhaps the things she'd gone through—had left their mark. Eve had once been a carefree soul. She loved to laugh and saw the good in every day. He wondered when she'd last let herself feel like that young girl.

"For stopping when you did. For saving me. For being there for my grandparents."

He swallowed several times, but the lump in his throat wouldn't go away. "They're good people. I still miss him terribly." Alfred and his wife had always been like grandparents to him, welcoming him into their home and their hearts with open arms.

When he'd first met Eve, they had immediately clicked. He'd spent a lot of time at Lourdes Estate and gotten to know her family well. They'd treated him like one of their own.

She pressed her fingers to her lips. "I still can't believe he's gone."

The pain in her eyes tore at his heart. Trent wondered if she felt guilty about not coming home sooner. Alfred wouldn't have wanted that.

"I know," he said quietly.

She reached over and clasped his hand. "He loved you, Trent. He always hoped..." She didn't finish, but he knew. Alfred had never stopped hoping he and Eve would reunite.

His breath hitched in his throat. "Yeah."

It was always like this between them. Even at Alfred's funeral, when she'd done everything in her power to keep their conversation as surface-level as possible, his reaction to her had been powerful. Would he love her for the rest of his life? If so, what kind of future could he have?

Trent pulled his gaze free and placed both hands on the steering wheel. Protecting her was his job and what Alfred had wanted. To do that, he'd have to find a way to distance himself from his emotions.

He maneuvered the SUV around before glancing at Eve. She stared out the windshield, no doubt replaying the events of the evening. What had started out as an exhausting trip home had quickly become a life-or-death struggle for survival.

Trent couldn't help but suspect that something cataclysmic for all of them was waiting to be discovered beyond the comfort of the SUV.

The paved drive that led to the house had been carved straight through the heart of the wilderness that Alfred Lourdes's family milled.

Trent thought about how close he'd once come to working full-time at the family's lumber mill. He'd spent the summer before their high school graduation earning money for college by working part-time in the mill. His father had thrown a fit when Trent had first broached the subject of working there permanently. His dad wanted better for his son.

He forced himself back to the present. "How are you holding up?"

She tried to put on a brave front, but her fear was almost palpable. "I'm okay."

"We'll catch him." Trent did his best to reassure her of something he wasn't so sure of himself.

She shook her head. "It's not that—well, not completely. I guess coming back here is already even harder than I thought."

The explosion from twelve years ago moved to the forefront of his thoughts. "I can imagine it won't be easy. It's still hard to accept that Christy is gone after all this time."

She seemed surprised. "You still think about her?"

"Every day. She was a good friend. What happened that night was terrible. It changed everything."

Eve didn't answer. It was as if an invisible door had slammed shut between them.

Trent was steering the SUV around a snake-like curve in the road when Eve suddenly grabbed his arm.

He stopped the SUV. "What's wrong?"

She pointed to the woods on her side. "There's someone out there."

He squinted through the darkness beyond her window and was ready to ask her again what she'd seen when he spotted it. A shadowy figure appeared at the edge of the woods, similar to the one who had attacked him and no doubt shot at them, but there was something different. The man who had attacked Trent had worn a hoodie pulled up over his knit cap. The man in the woods was dressed in black but wasn't wearing a jacket.

Before he had time to react, a gun barrel flashed. Trent grabbed Eve and shoved her down. Both passenger-side windows shattered, covering Eve with glass while shots continued to ricochet off the side of the vehicle.

Trent pressed the gas hard and the SUV shot forward. He kept as low as he could and still see enough to keep on the drive. If the shooter was the same person, then he was intent on killing Eve, and Trent had become collateral damage.

A mass of gunshots followed them until they were out of range. Trent rounded the next bend and braked as he tried to come up with a plan of action. Whether it was related to Alfred's suspicions or a killer from his past, the situation was deadly serious.

Eve sat up, her frightened eyes latching onto his.

Trent dragged in a breath. "Are you hurt?"

She shook her head.

"I have to go after him. Stay here." Telling himself she'd be safer out of sight in his vehicle, he nevertheless reached inside the glove box and pulled out his backup weapon. He checked to make sure it was loaded and handed it to her. "If anyone tries to break-in, don't hesitate."

Alfred had trained Eve in the proper way to use a weapon. She took the gun from him confidently.

"Lock up behind me." Trent exited the vehicle and waited until she'd engaged the locks.

The lights from the SUV and the full moon made it easy to spot the fleeing attacker's form, though Trent was too far away to see his face. The man glanced over his shoulder and noticed Trent. He fired again, forcing Trent to duck behind a tree.

Trent peeked out. He spotted the man and started after him once more, but the shooter had a definite head start.

The shooter disappeared into a group of densely populated trees. Trent slowed down, fearing a setup. Once he'd reached the trees he searched carefully, but there was no sign of the man.

Regret seeped through his body, and he doubled over, hands on his knees. He'd had the shooter in his sights and had let him get away. Again.

He swung back toward the direction in which the shooter had disappeared. If he kept going this way, it would eventually intersect with the road beyond where the police were searching.

A car's engine fired some distance away. Whoever was behind the attack was leaving.

Trent grabbed his phone and called Luke.

His friend answered before the first ring finished. "I heard the shots. Are you both safe?"

"He's getting away," Trent said, ignoring the question. He would answer it when he had time. "It sounds like the car was parked on this side of the road, hidden in the woods."

"I'll have my officers go after him. Hang on." Trent could hear Luke giving the order.

He started back to Eve. Even though he'd heard the car leaving, he couldn't let her out of his sight.

"Okay, they're pursuing. We're wrapping things up here," Luke said. "So far, it doesn't appear he left any viable evidence behind. I'm even more confused by the latest attack. He has to know we're out here. That's an awfully determined person. And we can't dismiss the fact that it doesn't match the Stalker's MO."

"I agree. At this point, I have no idea what's going on." And he was even more apprehensive about Eve's safety after multiple attempts on her life in one night.

"Stay with her, Trent," Luke added. "When I know anything, I'll be in touch." The call ended as he reached the SUV.

Eve unlocked the doors so he could get back in. "He got away?"

Trent nodded, putting the SUV in gear. "He did, but Luke has officers going after him. Hopefully, they'll be able to apprehend the shooter before he can get too far."

"I hope you're right."

He heard the doubt in her voice, and he certainly understood. So far, the shooter had attacked them three times in one night and they hadn't been able to contain him. The reckless aggression was concerning.

She offered him the handgun, but he stopped her. "Keep it. Just in case."

Eve tucked the small weapon into the waistband of her jeans and pulled her sweater over the top of it as they arrived at the gated entrance to the estate.

Trent punched in the code and they passed through two massive log gates, each engraved with the elegant trademark *L* for the family's name.

He glanced in the rearview mirror to confirm the gate closed while making sure no one had followed them inside.

Around the final curve in the drive, the mansion appeared before them, outside lights illuminating a rambling red brick, two-story home. Growing up with the family, Trent had heard all its stories, such as the time the river flooded the entire area so badly that there had been several feet of water inside the house. Through the years, other storms had given the place character marks. A fire around the turn of the century had destroyed nearly two-thirds of the interior of the house and had burned most of the forest around the estate. The family had rebuilt. Saplings had sprouted where the ruined ones had been as new life replaced the old. The forest and the house became stronger than before, much like those who lived within these walls.

Shortly before Alfred's death, Eve's grandmother had redone the landscaping, adding solar lights all around and shrubs that were native to the area. The manicured lawn was dotted with red and Norway maple trees like those milled by the family.

Trent pulled up to the front of the house and killed the engine. At his side, Eve seemed oblivious to his presence, staring at the house she'd once called home. One hand clutched her throat. Her mouth was slightly open as if in awe, or perhaps dread. Even without the attempts on her life, it was clear that her homecoming would not have been a happy one.

"Are you okay?" he asked quietly.

"I really don't know." The uncertainty on her face was hard to witness. "In all the times I've imagined returning, I've always been filled with apprehension. Now, after this—well, I think I've made a huge mistake by coming back here, Trent."

Even after what she'd gone through, hearing that she regretted coming was like a knife to his heart. "You're stronger than you think, Eve. You'll get through it. It's time you confronted your ghosts from the night of the explosion, once and for all."

She didn't seem nearly as certain as he was, but before she could reply, the front door opened. Jane Lourdes stood there with a troubled expression. She must have been watching for her granddaughter, but she wouldn't be expecting Eve to arrive with him. He wondered if she'd heard the shooting in the woods. Sound carried around the countryside.

The moment Jane got a good look at the damaged SUV, she flew down the steps to the passenger side.

Whatever Eve had been about to say was forgotten. She threw open the door and ran straight into her grandmother's arms.

Jane enveloped her granddaughter in her strong arms and held Eve close.

Trent got out and came around to where the two women embraced. "Sorry we're late, Jane."

"What on earth happened?" Jane's anxious gaze swept the vehicle covered in bullet holes.

Eve pulled away and shook her head as if warning Trent not to upset her grandmother.

"Eve ran into some weather-related trouble." He explained about her SUV going off the road, but left out the part about the shooting. Not that he'd be able to hide it for long when Jane was staring at the evidence on his vehicle.

Jane's piercing eyes bore into Trent's.

He held his breath, expecting a rush of questions, but Jane didn't push the matter.

"You're both soaked. Let's get you warm and dry." She kept her arm around Eve as they traversed the steps and went inside.

Trent followed them to the living room where most of the family had gathered to welcome Eve.

Jane's son Jacob rose as soon as they entered. "Good grief, Evie," he said. "You're all wet. Where've you been? We expected you some time ago." He wrapped her in a huge hug. "It doesn't matter. You're here now. Come sit by the fire."

As the baby of the family, Jacob was a mere ten years older than Eve. She'd told Trent many times how close she was with her youngest uncle.

"Betsy, can you get us some towels?" Jane asked her daughter-in-law.

"Of course." Samuel's wife hurried from the room.

Jacob dragged a chair close to the roaring flames in the massive stone fireplace. Eve collapsed into it and told her family the same story Trent had given Jane.

The family reunion that should have been filled with happiness was anything but.

Trent accepted a towel from Betsy, who draped the second one she carried over Eve's shoulders. He realized Samuel and Renee were both absent. "Where are your brother and sister?" he asked Jacob.

Samuel was the second-oldest child of Jane and Alfred after Melanie, and followed by Renee and then Jacob.

"I haven't seen Renee. She's probably out with Blake." Jacob rolled his eyes. Most of the family didn't approve of Renee's ex-husband and current boyfriend.

Trent wondered if Renee's absence was intentional. She seemed to have it out for her older sister and Eve for some reason.

"Samuel went to check on his horses. You know they're his pride and joy."

Jacob was right. Through the years, Samuel had bought some of the most sought-after Arabian show horses in the country. He loved working with them.

As if summoned, a drenched Samuel stepped inside. "What's going on, Trent? I saw your vehicle. Did you drive through a war zone on the way here?" Samuel meant it as a joke, but Eve flinched as if he'd struck her.

"It's a long story," Trent said.

Samuel seemed to think better of asking further questions.

Trent watched the strange family reunion play out while he wondered again if the attack tonight had come at the hands of a killer he'd been tracking, or as a result of something that dated back to the accident on the Lourdes property twelve years ago. Had Eve's return brought back more than just memories of that fateful night?

5

The warmth from the fire dried her clothes and hair, but a chill had seeped into Eve's very soul and refused to be dispelled by heat.

Eve glanced over her shoulder to where Trent stood by the door. He'd gone through so much to save her. She didn't want to think about what would have happened if Trent hadn't come along.

Her family's faces brought tears to her eyes. Despite everything, she'd missed them. Missed being part of their lives through the years, especially her grandmother.

Gran caressed her cheek. "Good. You're warming up and your color has returned." She pulled up a chair beside Eve's. "We're all excited to have you home. It's been too long, Eve." Gran's voice cracked, and she impatiently swiped a tear from her cheek.

The sight of her grandmother crying tore Eve apart. She hadn't realized how much Gran had missed her.

"It's been such a blessing having the family here with me since your grandpa passed. Betsy helped me get your old room ready for your visit." Gran forced a smile. "Everything is how you left it."

"I didn't realize everyone was staying here." The idea puzzled Eve. Jacob had a house in an affluent part of Winter Lake. Samuel and Betsy lived in the next town over. As far as Eve knew, only Renee stayed at the estate.

"My boys have been here since before the funeral." She smiled at her children. "It's good to have life in the house again. Alfred would be proud of the way our sons have been taking care of me."

Eve squeezed her grandmother's hand. "I'm glad you aren't lonely. How is everyone taking the news of selling the estate?"

"They know this is what is best," Jane said as if it were a real answer.

Jacob patted his mother's arm and Eve noticed the tattoo he'd gotten on his hand many years ago. He'd gotten into so much trouble when Grandpa Alfred found out about it. "We want Mom to be happy. It's been hard since Dad passed."

Samuel's mouth thinned, but he kept his attention on the fire. Since he was the oldest son, Eve wondered about her uncle's true opinion of selling the family property.

Renee's absence was no doubt a conscious snub. Even when Eve and her mother and father lived here, Renee seemed to hold a grudge against them for some reason.

"You must be exhausted after the long drive and the accident." Her grandmother kissed her cheek. "Come, child, let me show you to your room. There will be plenty of time to catch up tomorrow."

Eve rose on unsteady legs. The world around her swam, and she pressed her hand to her forehead.

Eve hugged each of her family members before Gran helped her to the door where Trent stood talking to Luke on his phone. The conversation ended as they approached.

"I should be going too," he told her.

After everything she and Trent had been through in a few hours, she found that she didn't want to let him go. No one but Eve, Trent, and the police knew about the attacks on the road. She would have to tell her family eventually, but for the time being, simply being back in the home where she saw her grandfather and her father everywhere—that was all she could take.

Trent hesitated, then leaned over and kissed her cheek. "I will see you in the morning."

"Let me walk you out," she told him. "Gran, I'll be right back."

She and Trent walked without speaking. He opened the door and stepped out into the dreary night.

Eve followed him out and closed the door behind her. The darkness beyond the house lights gave her the creeps. Was the criminal still out there somewhere waiting for another chance to strike?

"You'll call me when you know something, right?" Eve pushed back strands of hair from her face. The cold seemed to pierce right through her clothes.

"I will," he promised. He held out his hand. "Give me your phone and I'll put in my number. If anything comes up, or if you just want to talk, call me." She gave it to him, and he tapped on the screen, then handed it back. "Try not to worry, Eve. You're safe here. You've got your uncles to keep an eye on things. And if you need anything, I'm right through those trees at the caretaker's cabin. I can be here in a couple of minutes."

Eve wanted to believe him, but it had been a horrible night and she was scared to death. Trent made her feel less afraid. She grabbed his hand when he started to leave.

His expression softened when he saw her panic. Without a word, Trent pulled her into a hug. Her head rested against his chest. The rhythmic beat of his heart was as steady as the man himself.

But she couldn't lean on Trent forever. It wasn't fair to him. With a deep sigh, Eve pulled away. "Thank you. For everything." She stroked his cheek. No matter what, she would always care about Trent. It was as if he were part of her DNA. She couldn't change that.

"It really is good to have you back." Trent let her go and descended the steps in that confident way of his. He climbed into his battered SUV and waved as he drove past.

Eve rubbed her arms, feeling vulnerable. Someone wanted her

dead. She still couldn't wrap her head around the idea of anybody having so much anger toward her. She fumbled with the door, her hands shaking. She peered over her shoulder before rushing inside, then slammed the door and snapped the lock into place.

"Honey, are you okay?" Gran crossed the room to Eve. "You're safe here, child."

Safe. Eve struggled not to scoff. She was anything but safe. Yet the last thing Eve wanted was to pile onto her grandmother's troubles. If Gran knew everything Eve had gone through, she would blame herself for calling her granddaughter home.

Eve forced a smile. "I guess I'm still a little rattled."

Gran put her arm around Eve's shoulders. "I'm so sorry you had to go through that, Eve." She glanced around. "Where are your bags?"

Eve couldn't tell her they were part of a crime scene. "I left them in my vehicle. After everything that happened, I just wanted to get out of there. I'll have Trent take me over to get them tomorrow."

Her grandmother didn't question her answer. "I have something you can sleep in tonight. Let's get you settled." She kept her arm around Eve's shoulders as they ascended the sweeping marble staircase.

Childhood memories flooded in. How Eve used to slide down the banister despite her mother's warnings. That time she'd ridden her sled down the stairs, much to Grandpa Alfred's delight.

Gran opened the door to Eve's old bedroom and stepped inside.

Crossing that threshold was next to impossible. The last moments here with her friend Christy slammed into her. They'd been listening to music and talking about their plans for the upcoming weekend. Suddenly Christy hadn't felt well and had wanted to go home.

"You know what, I think one of your old nightgowns is still here in one of the drawers." Her grandmother's sweet voice broke the spell of the heartbreaking memory.

Eve gazed around the room without responding. Everything about the place was exactly as it had been when she'd lived there. Almost as if it had been waiting through the years for her return, right down to the stuffed teddy bear from her father on the bed. All the photos on the wall were the same. Even back then, Eve had loved taking pictures.

"Ah, yes. Here you go." Gran held up an old pink gown with kittens printed on it.

Eve chuckled. "You kept it all these years?"

"Of course. I figured when you did decide to come home, it would make it easier if everything was as you left it." Her grandmother moved with the grace of the dancer she'd once been. Before her marriage, she'd had a promising career as a ballerina in New York City. Then Alfred had swept her off her feet and she'd never looked back. Still, Eve could tell the loss of her husband had taken its toll. Gran's shoulders were stooped, and there were dark circles under her eyes that hinted at quite a few sleepless nights.

Eve spoke to her grandmother every week. They'd shared their grief since Grandpa Alfred's passing. When Gran had told her she wanted to sell the estate, Eve hadn't fully bought into the idea.

Now, seeing the weight of the world on her grandmother's shoulders, Eve believed her.

Gran kissed her cheek. "Get some sleep, honey. It's good to have you back home."

With another sweet smile, her grandmother quietly closed the door and left Eve alone with the haunts of the past.

Sleep wasn't going to be possible—at least not for a while. She wandered around the room, too keyed up to rest. Being back at Lourdes Mansion was harder than she'd expected. Sure, there were fragments of horrible memories from the night of the explosion, but they were outnumbered by the good ones that reflected eighteen years of love and happiness with her grandparents, her parents, and her uncles who'd doted on her growing up.

Tears burned at the back of her eyes. It had been an emotional day. Gran was right. She should rest.

Eve placed Trent's gun on the nightstand, then scooped up the nightgown and took it into the adjoining bathroom. Like the bedroom, everything was exactly as she'd left it that last night. The warm shower melted the last bit of cold away from her skin. Eve slipped into the gown and snuggled in under the pink flannel sheets, the fresh scent of lavender laundry detergent wafting around her head. She pulled the thick comforter up around her chin. She was home.

And someone wanted her dead.

Eve extinguished the light. Her body ached from the strain of the accident and her head pounded, yet her mind refused to shut down. She relived every second of what had happened, feeling the same fear and adrenaline she'd experienced then.

"I'm safe here," she whispered, wanting to trust it as she listened to the unfamiliar sounds of the house. The quiet conversation coming from downstairs had ended.

Guilt wrapped its spindly fingers around her heart like it had so many times. She should have set aside her fears and been there for her grandparents. She'd lost so many years with her grandmother, and precious time she'd never get back with Grandpa Alfred.

Eve rolled over on her side and closed her eyes. "Come on. Let's get this over with." And she did. The past—good and bad—swallowed her up.

"No, please no." She tossed fitfully in her sleep as the darkness closed in. "Please. Leave me alone." But it continued to grow until it enveloped her, carrying her back to the moment in time she'd avoided for so long.

"No." She wasn't ready. Eve fought with everything inside to open her eyes, to escape the darkness. She bolted upright in the bed. Her heart pounded out a frenzied beat as the remnants of the nightmare faded and her childhood room replaced it. She was home at Lourdes Mansion. Not at the garage following the explosion. Struggling to breathe, to hear, to understand.

Eve tossed the covers back and sat up. The last thing she wanted was to be alone, with the nightmare still so fresh.

Dark shadows clung to everything in the room. It was barely light out. She dressed in the jeans and sweater she'd worn the night before and went downstairs.

Everyone was still sleeping. She ventured to the kitchen and started much-needed coffee.

If the dream were any indication, returning to the estate had been a huge mistake. She should have recommended someone else to help with the property. The excitement she'd heard in Gran's voice at the prospect of having Eve home again had made her reluctant to disappoint her sweet grandmother.

The sooner she took the necessary photos and went over the items her grandmother wanted to sell with the property, the sooner she'd be able to return to Syracuse. And pray the nightmare wouldn't follow her home.

Outside the kitchen window, pinks and reds began to creep across the sky, heralding the new day. The outdoors called to her. Eve grabbed her coffee and camera. She'd take a walk to clear her head. The property around the house was surrounded by a six-foot stone wall, so she'd be safe.

Eve chose a jacket from the coat rack that she assumed was her grandmother's and stepped out into the morning chill. A thick fog still hung in the air, distorting the sounds of the property. She left the porch and headed away from the restored garage where the explosion had taken place. Merely being near it filled her with apprehension.

She'd loved growing up on the grounds. The entire estate had been one big playground. She'd spent hours creating adventures. Back then, her dad had been a huge part of her life. He encouraged her imagination, and they'd spent hours together exploring the property or riding horses. Eve had loved him with all her heart. The way he'd left without so much as a word to her still cut deep.

Another round of light rain had begun to fall. Eve pulled up the hood of the jacket and shoved aside her father's betrayal.

Eve concentrated on the positive aspects of the property, of which there were many. The view from the front of the barns resembled a winter wonderland when the snow came. As she took in the serene beauty, darkness from the past crowded in once more. She'd experienced it for days before she'd made the trip. A warning that the things she'd been told about the explosion were nothing close to the truth.

She headed for the back of the house. The woods surrounding the place had always been the perfect place to clear her head. The trees had a magical feel. The walking path Grandpa Alfred had cut through the trees would be beautiful at this time of the year with the spring flowers coming in. The property was home to many deer. Perhaps she'd be lucky enough to see some that morning.

As she entered the trees, the temperature dropped considerably. She realized in horror that she'd forgotten to bring the gun with her. A shiver slipped down her spine—a feeling of being watched. Was it real, or merely remnants of the night before?

She gathered the jacket closer and walked at a faster pace. Morning shadows created a twilight appearance in the woods, making it hard to see much.

A twig snapped behind her. Eve jerked toward the noise. In the semidarkness, something moved.

A man wearing a ski mask and dark clothing emerged. Just like the one from the night before.

She screamed. If this was the same man, he'd breached the high walls around the property to get to her. She wasn't safe at all.

With her breath coming in painful gasps, she ran as fast as she could, arms pumping at her sides. Eve glanced over her shoulder. He was gaining on her. She lost her footing on the damp leaves and fell hard.

"No!" Eve flipped onto her back and searched the twilight. *Where did he go?*

A shadow fell across her.

She screamed and fought for her life. She wasn't about to die without doing everything she could to save herself.

"Eve, it's me." Trent grabbed her flaying hands in his. The familiar sound of his voice reached past the terror, and she stopped struggling.

"Trent?" Relief flooded her body. "Did you see him?"

"Did I see who?"

"The man in the mask. He was here, Trent. He chased me."

Trent helped her to her feet. "I didn't see anyone, but I heard you scream and came as fast as I could. What happened?"

"I came out to take a look at the property and to clear my head. There was a man in a mask waiting for me in the woods." Eve shuddered. "I was so scared, Trent. I think he wanted to kill me." She ran a hand over her face. "If you hadn't heard me scream, I'd be dead."

6

Someone had come after Eve within the walls of the estate. Trent had believed she would be safe, but the attack proved otherwise. He should never have let her out of his sight. As much as he wanted to go after the perp, he couldn't leave Eve alone.

She pulled away. "Are you sure you didn't see anyone? He was right here."

"I saw Samuel heading to his car for work, but that's all." Trent had been going to the house when Samuel had driven by. The brazenness of the perp's latest attempt on Eve's life shook him to his core. "I set up some security cameras around the place when your grandfather hired me to find out who was illegally trapping on the family property." He pulled up the camera coverage on his phone and reviewed the feed.

"There's nothing," she said, disappointment evident in her voice.

"That's impossible. There's a camera close to this location. It should have picked up everything."

Together they headed to the camera. He hated lying to Eve about why the cameras were there, but Alfred had been specific. He didn't want Eve to know she might be in danger. The cameras had been set up under the guise of monitoring illegal trapping. It was the cover story he and Alfred had created to explain Trent's lengthy stay at the estate, while he actually investigated the long-ago explosion.

Trent saw the damage to the camera before they reached it. It lay on the ground beneath the tree where it had been installed.

"Someone smashed it." Eve pivoted toward him, her eyes huge and unsettled.

Muddy footprints were everywhere. Someone had been there, and had wanted to make sure they didn't know who it was.

"Let's get you out of here." He took her arm and started for an old caretaker's cabin on the property where he was camped out temporarily.

Trent understood Eve hadn't wanted to worry her family, but with the new attack, he would need the family's cooperation to help keep her safe.

"I don't understand what he wants," she said. "Do you really think this is connected to the serial killer you were tracking before you left the force?"

He was far from convinced. With the differences in MO, Trent wondered if it might be someone trying to make him think it was the killer. "To be honest, I have no idea."

She frowned. "But it could be."

"Yes, it's possible."

She peeked over her shoulder as if expecting another attack. "But you can't be sure because not everything fits the killer's usual method."

"Exactly. While it's not unheard of for a serial killer to change it up, this one has been fairly consistent in the past."

She hugged her arms around her body. "I don't understand any of this. Why would this killer target me? I haven't lived here in years. And if it isn't the Stalker, then who is it?"

The caretaker's cabin peeked through the trees in front of them.

"You aren't really here because of some illegal trapping, are you?" she said, and stopped walking to face him.

While he considered how much to tell her, something at the front of the cabin caught his attention. The door stood ajar. It had been closed when he left the house.

"Wait here," he whispered, grabbing his gun.

The sight of the weapon sent new alarm flashing in Eve's eyes. "Trent, he could be in there."

"I'll be fine." He appreciated that she was worried about him, but if the man who had tried to hurt Eve was still inside, Trent wasn't going to miss the chance to capture him.

He edged toward the open door and listened carefully. Not a single sound from inside. Trent nudged the door open enough to pass through. His gaze panned around the living and dining room. There was nothing out of place, no sign anyone but him had been inside.

When he stepped further into the cabin, Trent noticed the back door standing wide open. Someone had been inside the cabin and had left in a hurry. The question was—what had the intruder hoped to find? He wondered if what had happened in the woods was a distraction to get him away from the cabin so it could be searched, but nothing was missing.

Trent shoved the gun back into his pocket and went back outside to where Eve waited.

"Whoever was there is gone now," he told her.

Her brows drew together. "Why search your house?"

There was only one thing he could think of, and it blew the serial killer connection out of the running. If someone had broken in for the information Alfred had given him, then the intrusion was far more personal.

Though he'd been through the document several times, Trent still didn't understand the significance.

"I'm calling Luke. He needs to know about this." Luke would send a crime scene unit out to search for trace evidence left behind by whoever had been in the cabin. Trent doubted they'd find any.

He pulled the phone from his pocket to call Luke but before he placed the call, it rang. Luke was calling him.

He raised an eyebrow at Eve and answered. "Good morning, Luke."

"Hey. How are things there?"

"Not good. I was just about to call you." He filled his former partner in on the morning's events.

"I'm on my way," Luke said. "We're ten minutes out."

Trent sensed there was more that Luke wasn't saying. "What is it?"

Luke's hesitation spoke volumes. "I'll tell you when we get there." The call ended.

"What's wrong?" Eve asked.

"I'm not sure. Luke's on his way. For now, it's best if we stay out here until they've had a chance to process the place." Following procedure would help him work through the situation rationally, so he continued with the next part of the process—getting the statement. "Did anyone know you were taking a walk?"

"No. As far as I know, no one else was up."

He remembered seeing Samuel leave for work. "Actually, someone was. There's a chance your uncle might have seen someone parked on the road." Trent grabbed his phone again and called Samuel.

Once he'd explained that he believed someone might have been on the property earlier, Samuel's concern became clear. "Unbelievable. Now that you mention it, I did pass a car on the road. I didn't think anything of it, though."

"What did the car look like?"

"Dark blue, or maybe black—I'm not sure." He could hear Samuel second-guessing himself.

"Did you catch a glimpse of the driver?" Trent prayed Samuel could remember details about the person behind the wheel. They needed something to break their way.

"To be honest, I didn't really pay attention," Samuel admitted. "I was on the phone with my assistant going over meetings for the day.

I'm sorry, Trent. Do you think this has something to do with the illegal trapping taking place around the property?"

Trent hated not telling Samuel the truth, but the fewer people who knew that they were searching for more than an illegal trapper, the more likely it was that they'd be able to catch the real culprit. Trent had seen it time and time again. Perps who thought no one was onto them got sloppy—and that was when they got caught.

On the other hand, Samuel had the right to know what was going on with his family's property. But Trent didn't want to tell him over the phone, or without Eve's permission.

"Someone was definitely on the grounds, which means they had to climb the fence to get here," he explained, watching Eve's face. She was probably one more bad thing away from leaving again, and he couldn't stand that. Keeping her safe was the most important thing, and he couldn't do that if she was in Syracuse. At some point, after everything was over, he wanted them to talk—really talk—about what had torn them apart.

Samuel groaned in frustration. "All right. Keep me posted."

Once the call ended, Trent said to Eve, "We're going to have to tell your family the truth about last night and today. We can't keep them in the dark. This affects everyone. Is there a reason you don't want to tell them?"

She bit her lip. "Gran's been through so much already, and it's stressful enough for her to be selling the family home. I don't want her thinking she's put my life in danger by asking for my help."

He certainly understood, but Jane was strong. He'd witnessed that strength in the months following Alfred's passing. "Still, at some point, she'll have to be told, along with the rest of your family."

Eve reluctantly agreed. "I know. I guess I'm hoping we can figure this out before it comes to that."

Trent didn't want to tell her that he had a feeling uncovering the attacker's identity wasn't going to be easy. The person coming after Eve wouldn't give up, and they had no idea whether he was connected to the Roadside Stalker or something from the past.

The sound of approaching vehicles pulled his attention to the drive. "That'll be Luke."

Multiple police vehicles had arrived with their lights flashing. Luke parked his SUV by the cabin and got out, along with several officers. Once Luke had given orders to his people, he came over to where Trent and Eve waited.

"Sounds like you've had another scare," he told Eve. "They're starting to pile up."

Her weary face reflected the turmoil she'd been through. "Yes they are. I still can't believe this."

"Anything missing inside?" Luke asked Trent.

Trent shook his head. "No, nothing. I'm not sure what they were after."

Luke had Eve recount the events in the woods.

She took a step closer to Trent as she spoke.

Luke's grim expression revealed his opinion once she'd finished. "This guy is becoming more determined, which makes him extremely dangerous. I'd like to station some of my officers outside the wall around the property. I'll need the family's permission."

Eve promptly gave it. "Do it. If anyone has a problem, I'll tell them I said it was okay."

"This is serious, Eve," Luke said. "Everyone in the family could be in danger. You need to tell them the truth."

Eve nodded. "Trent thinks so too."

"I can speak to them with you," Trent offered.

She gave him a small, grateful smile.

"I spoke briefly to Samuel," Trent told Luke. "He was leaving the property when everything went down. He noticed a car, but not the driver. It was a dark-color sedan, like the one Eve saw last night and the one that's been lurking around the place. Did you get any useful evidence from Eve's car?"

Luke watched his people work through the open door. "Not a single usable print. No trace DNA. Whoever did this is smart. He knows how to keep from being detected." Luke's words settled around Trent uncomfortably. "We did pull a single bullet from the crime scene near the house. It fits a 9mm. You know how common those are."

"Do you still think this is related to the Stalker case?" Eve asked.

Luke took his time answering. "I'm not ready to rule it out entirely, but it is becoming less and less likely. The Stalker never used a gun before, and according to the single witness we have, the Stalker didn't disguise his appearance. This could be a random attack, or someone wanting to settle a score."

"I know we've already asked, but can you think of any reason why someone might hold a grudge against you? Anything, even if it seems insignificant."

"No, there's nothing—" She stopped, her frown deepening.

Trent wondered if she was remembering something from the night of the explosion. Something that might explain why someone wanted her dead.

7

A shadowy memory teased at the back of her mind, refusing to be set free. Every time she came close to remembering, her heart threatened to go ballistic. What terrible thing waited for her in the past?

The things she remembered from that night were mere snippets, like a grainy old movie that didn't make sense.

Several officers who had been searching the woods for evidence headed their way.

"Anything?" Luke asked the sergeant in charge.

"There are lots of footprints, but with the continued rain they're so badly disintegrated we can't distinguish one set from another, or get any clear impressions to take to the lab. They led to the property wall. We found imprints that suggested the perp had a ladder with him to scale it."

Luke rubbed a hand across his forehead. "I was afraid of that."

The lead officer of the crime scene unit joined them. "We pulled a few fingerprints from the rear door, but I'm guessing they'll be a match for yours, Trent."

Eve's attacker had worn a ski mask to hide his face. Though she hadn't seen his hands, she doubted he would be careless enough not to wear gloves.

"Appreciate it." Luke watched his officers return to their vehicles and leave. "Until we catch this guy, I don't want you walking around outside alone, Eve."

She'd known Luke for many years and had never seen him so somber before. "I understand."

"I'll get my people set up outside the property as soon as possible," Luke said to Trent. "Once they're in place I'll let you know."

"Thanks, Luke," Trent said.

Luke nodded. "Oh, and Eve, I've got your suitcase and purse in my vehicle." He brought her bags out from the SUV. Trent took her suitcase while Luke handed Eve her purse. "Be careful, both of you. We don't know where this guy is going to strike next."

With his words of warning still ringing in her ears, Eve watched Luke climb behind the wheel.

"I'm sure your grandmother will have seen the law enforcement presence by now," Trent said as the police vehicles drove away. "She'll be concerned. We should probably get you home."

Before he'd taken a single step, she stopped him.

Trent gazed at her in question. The concern on his face was all for her and so unmerited. She'd taken the coward's way out, all those years ago—running away instead of talking to him. Trent deserved so much more.

Eve tried to clear away the lump in her throat. "Do you mind if we stay here for just a little longer?" Her nerves were shot. She wasn't ready to face Gran yet, but spending time with Trent was bittersweet. It reminded Eve that when she went back to Syracuse, she'd be leaving a piece of her heart behind.

His expression softened. He reached out and touched her cheek.

Trent had grown up from that lanky young boy she'd loved to the strong protector who stood before her. There was no denying the sparks from their youth were still there, waiting to be reignited. She couldn't let that happen, couldn't break both their hearts again.

She stepped back awkwardly, and his hand dropped to his side. She didn't miss the way his jaw tightened.

"Want some coffee?" he asked in a tight voice.

Eve slowly smiled. "That would be great."

He walked beside her to the small cabin that had once belonged to the family's groundskeeper.

Gran had told her over the past few years they'd been using a service to maintain the property. It was no longer necessary to have someone on-site.

Trent held the door open for her. "Have a seat. I'll make the coffee."

He disappeared into the little kitchen. Too on edge to sit, Eve followed him and watched him take out two cups, then prepare the beverages.

He brought out sugar and cream as if they'd last had coffee yesterday instead of twelve years ago.

Once it finished brewing, he handed her a cup.

"Thank you." She accepted the cup from him, grateful for its warmth.

Trent took a sip and leaned back against the stove while she pondered the changes she saw in him.

"Grandpa Alfred told me you started your own private investigation firm. What made you leave the force? I thought you'd always wanted to be a detective."

His expression closed off.

She wished the question back. She had no right to ask him about his life now. "Sorry, that's none of my business."

He ran a hand over his face, making a clear effort to relax. "No, it's okay. Actually, it was the Stalker case that sealed it for me." He stared into his coffee cup with a pensive expression. "Luke and I ended up with the case. A twenty-eight-year-old woman had disappeared."

"What happened?"

"Her dad reported her missing. He met us over at her house where she lived alone. The first thing we noticed was a pile of mail. There was a letter among the rest that grabbed our attention right away.

The envelope was blank and contained a single piece of paper with cut-out letters." His intense gaze met hers. "'Soon you will be mine.' He wrote the same thing to every single victim."

As hard as it was to talk about, she had to know. "How did he kill them?"

"With a knife. Up close."

It was obvious the case had become personal for him. "Is that why you left the force?" she asked softly, and saw the truth before he could answer. "Because you couldn't solve it."

He flinched. "It was. I still see the last victim every time I close my eyes."

"Oh, Trent." Eve set down her cup and went to him. "I'm so sorry." She entwined her pinky finger with his as she had so many times when they were dating.

"Thanks," he murmured, his voice thick with emotion. "She was the youngest of the victims and, to my knowledge, the last. Samantha was a good person who only wanted to help people. And she ran into a monster."

Eve wished she could make it better for him.

"I promised her parents we would bring her home safely." The haunted look in his eyes held her captive. "I should never have done that. Luke and I spent hours searching for some clue that would give us the killer's identity. The case consumed me. I knew I was heading down a dark road." His mouth twisted. "Your grandfather saw it. He took me aside and told me I had two choices. I could either live in the past and be consumed by it, or I could move forward. Though it was hard to leave the force, it was time. I started my own business. I never told Alfred, but in my free time, I continue to work the case because I made a promise to the family. I will see the Roadside Stalker behind bars."

He'd had a hero's heart for as long as she could remember. She wasn't surprised that he would go to such lengths to fulfill a promise. And he would do everything in his power to make sure she was safe.

"You saved my life again. I owe you so much," she said. The words seemed inadequate.

"I'd do anything for you, Eve. You know that."

She did. Eve was reminded again of how their lives might have been if she'd stayed and fought through her trauma instead of running away. Her chest grew tight. Suddenly, it hurt to breathe.

Her phone buzzed and she jumped back, the spell broken. Eve pulled it from her pocket.

"It's my grandmother." She cleared her throat and answered the call.

"Eve, what on earth is going on? I saw the police cars over at the cabin. Are you safe?"

"We're both fine, Gran," Eve said, trying to keep her voice steady and reassuring. "I'm with Trent now. We're on our way back to the house. I'll explain everything once we get there."

"Okay, hon. I'll talk to you soon." The call ended.

Eve shoved the phone back into her jeans. "I need to go. She's worried."

"That's understandable," he said, his voice rough.

They stepped outside into a light mist. At least the heavier rain had let up.

Trent locked the cabin door. "To be safe, let's take the SUV. I'll feel better not being completely exposed." He placed her suitcase in the back and opened the passenger door to his battered SUV.

As they started toward the house, Eve remembered her vehicle. She'd all but forgotten about the crash. "Did Luke tell you where my car ended up?"

"It was towed to the police lab for further tests. I asked Luke to have it sent to Rusty's to be cleaned and repaired. Rusty will fix it up for a fair price."

Rusty Matters had been in their grade in school. He'd always loved working on cars and had joined his uncle's repair business after graduating. A few years back, Rusty had bought out his uncle.

Eve was touched by Trent's thoughtfulness. "I appreciate that."

He brought the SUV to a stop in front of the house and shifted in his seat. "You're doing the right thing by telling her. She needs to hear the whole story, Eve. She can handle it."

As much as she wanted to protect her grandmother, Trent was right. Gran was strong. She'd manage whatever danger came her way.

"You're right. She can."

He squeezed her arm. The smile on his face faded as their eyes locked.

The urgency facing them moved to the background. It was just the two of them and a wealth of things that needed to be said. And she couldn't get a single one of them out.

Trent cleared his throat and looked away. A second later he left the SUV, and she released a huge breath.

Trent opened her door and stepped back to let her out. Together, they walked up to the porch without a word.

Before Trent could reach for the handle, the door swung open. Aunt Renee's former husband and the man she was currently seeing, Blake Wilkins, stepped out.

Blake stopped short upon noticing them. "Oh, hey. I didn't realize anyone was out here." He quickly stuffed something into his pocket. "Renee told me you were back."

No "Welcome home." No "How've you been?" Not a single emotion. There was always a little something about Blake that gave Eve the creeps.

Neither Blake nor Renee had been around the previous night when Eve had arrived. The last time she'd seen Renee had been at Grandpa

Alfred's funeral, and Blake hadn't been there. According to Gran, he had started coming around a few weeks before.

When Eve and her mother had left Lourdes Mansion, Renee and Blake were still married. They divorced shortly afterward. According to Gran, they continued to talk off and on. Gran had made no bones about her dislike of Blake, who couldn't seem to hold on to a job and had mooched off Renee for years.

"Hello, Blake. Are you going somewhere?" she asked.

"What? No. Getting some air." His mouth hardened, and he started down the steps, grumbling "See you around" over his shoulder.

Eve watched him hurry away.

"That was strange," Trent said beside her. "What's he so jumpy about?"

"I have no idea." She'd never really cared for Blake. It wasn't because of anything that she could really pinpoint, merely a feeling.

Putting Blake out of her mind, Eve stepped inside the house with Trent.

Gran must have heard them come in. She and Betsy emerged from the kitchen and closed the space between them. Her grandmother enveloped Eve in an embrace. "I was so worried when I saw all those police vehicles. Are you sure you're all right?"

"I'm fine, Gran." Eve let go of her grandmother and tried to find the words to express the nightmare she'd gone through since arriving, without terrifying Gran.

"Something happened in the woods earlier," Trent began for her, and she was grateful. "Is there someplace we can go to talk in private?"

Gran's concern for Eve was immediately replaced by alarm. "Yes, of course. Alfred's office." She led the way to Grandpa's old study.

Gran closed the door and waited along with Betsy.

How could Eve even begin to explain everything?

Eve reached for her grandmother's hand. "Come and sit with me, both of you. This is not going to be easy."

She and Gran went to the brown leather sofa near the fireplace while Betsy slipped into the overstuffed chair that Grandpa Alfred had been fond of.

The room was filled with memories. Eve swallowed hard.

"What's going on, Eve?" Gran prompted. "Why were those police officers on the property?" She stared at Eve's mud-stained jeans.

Eve took a deep breath and told the woman who had been her rock about the frightening events of the previous night and the attack that morning.

"Oh, dear Lord," Betsy exclaimed.

"Why would someone want to hurt you?" Gran shifted from Eve to Trent. "What is this about?"

Trent claimed the chair beside Gran. "We're not sure yet. Luke and I are investigating. I think I've seen the car that ran Eve off the road around recently." He omitted its possible connection to a serial killer. Eve understood there was no need to bring up the possibility when Luke and Trent weren't convinced it was true.

"Oh, honey." Gran put her arm around Eve's shoulders and held her close. "Why didn't you tell me?"

"I didn't want to frighten you." Eve did her best to reassure her grandmother that she was okay, even though she was far from it.

"This has to be some type of misunderstanding," Betsy said. "Why would anyone target you?"

"I don't know." Once more, the past teased her with what she couldn't recall. Something dreadful was buried in her memories. Something Eve wasn't sure she was ready to face.

"Luke will have officers stationed outside of the wall, and I'm close." Trent held Eve's gaze. "For now, please don't leave the house without me. I know you have work to do, but I'd like to be part of it, as a precaution."

If Trent thought she needed a constant bodyguard, the situation was even more dire than she'd thought.

"If it's okay with you, I'd like to speak with the rest of the family and let them know," Trent told the women.

"All right, but Samuel isn't here," Gran said. "He's gone into the office for a meeting."

"I'll give him a call later on," Trent told them.

Gran rose. "Jacob and Renee were having breakfast. I don't know where Blake is." Her mouth thinned at the mention of her former son-in-law. She started for the kitchen with Betsy while Eve and Trent followed.

The wealth of memories from the happier times she'd spent there were all around. Making breakfast together with her mother and Gran. The special Christmas cinnamon rolls Gran let her assist with even though she was probably more in the way than a help, yet Gran never complained. Eve would watch them rise and couldn't wait for the first bite of warm roll.

"There she is," Jacob said, and rose from his seat to give her a hug. "How are you feeling after your ordeal yesterday?" His smile faded when he got a good look at Eve. "What's wrong?"

"Someone tried to kill Eve this morning," Betsy blurted.

"No way." He seemed to be struggling to take in what Betsy said. "How? Why?"

Trent filled him in. "Have either you or Renee noticed anything unusual around the property? Anyone hanging around who doesn't belong?"

"No, there's been no one," Jacob promptly confirmed. "Did your security cameras capture anything?"

Trent shook his head. "The one near where the attack took place today was damaged, which makes me think the attacker has been on the property before and knows about the cameras. He disabled that one so we couldn't see him." Trent glanced toward where Renee was watching the discussion with only mild interest. "What about you, Renee? Have you seen anything unusual?"

Renee sniffed disdainfully and pushed back her silver-blonde hair. "Why would I know what's taking place in the woods? I detest them. But maybe someone's trying to tell you something, Eve." She smiled nastily.

"That's enough, Renee," Gran said sternly. "Eve is my granddaughter and this is her home."

Renee shrugged and picked up her coffee cup.

"What about Blake?" Trent pressed. "What's he been up to this morning?"

Renee appeared bored. "How would I know? You'd have to ask him."

"I will," Trent assured her with a hard edge to his voice.

"Whatever I can do to help, let me know," Jacob said. "I'm not letting anything happen to our Evie."

Eve smiled at his childhood nickname for her. "Thank you." She squeezed his hand, glad to have him and Uncle Samuel around. They'd been her protectors growing up.

Trent checked the time on his phone. "I've got to go. I have a conference call with a client in ten minutes. Walk me to the door, Eve?" He clasped Eve's hand as they left the room. Holding it felt as natural as it had in the past.

"I meant what I said," he told her. "Please don't leave the house without me until we catch this criminal."

"I won't. I promise." She made the signal for crossing her heart to lighten the moment.

He opened the front door, then gazed silently at her, and once more it was hard to breathe normally.

The sound of her phone ringing made her jump. Eve laughed nervously. "I guess I'm a little on edge. She pulled the phone from her jeans pocket. "I'm sure it's Mom."

Except that the caller ID read *Unknown*.

Eve swiped to answer the call. "Hello?"

Background noise screamed into her ear. She held the phone a little away.

"Hello? Is anyone there?"

More screeching sounds and then a voice spoke, distorted beyond all recognition.

"Leave now. Or die."

8

Eve dropped the phone, and it clattered against the marble floor of the entryway. She was close to hyperventilating.

"Eve? Who was that?" Trent scooped up the phone. "Hello? Is anyone there?"

There was no reply.

Trent grasped Eve's shoulders. "What did he say?"

She was shivering. "He told me if I don't leave, I'll die."

Trent closed the door and locked it before ushering Eve into the living room. "Did you recognize the voice?"

She'd suffered a terrible shock and it showed on her pale features. "No, his voice was distorted, like he was using some type of app to disguise it. I'm not even sure it was a man."

This changes everything. The Stalker had never done anything like it before. So who had made the threatening phone call, and why? Was someone trying to mimic the Stalker's actions, or at least wanted them to think it was him?

But the call made things far more personal. How did they have her number? The Stalker wouldn't have known it if she'd been selected at random.

Her purse had been searched in her SUV. He could have somehow found her number from seeing her address on Eve's driver's license. But if this was the Stalker, why hadn't he just taken the license as he had in previous crimes?

"I'd like to call Luke and see if he can trace where the call originated.

Is that all right with you?"

Eve nodded, then absently moved to the fireplace that still held embers from the evening before.

Trent waited for Luke to pick up and prayed he would be able to protect her.

"Has something else happened?" Luke asked in a tight voice.

Trent filled in his partner. "Can you try to find out where the call originated?"

"We'll do our best. But if he's disguising his voice, you know the chances of him using a phone we can track are slim."

"I realize it's a long shot, but it's all I can think of to do," Trent said.

"As soon as I know something, I'll call, but this keeps getting more and more bizarre," Luke said.

"What do you mean?" Trent asked. "Did you find something else."

"I told you there weren't any prints or DNA evidence left behind in Eve's car, but there was something. A single hair." Luke paused, and Trent tried to brace himself for the tidal wave coming his way. "It matches the one we found in Samantha's car."

Trent's blood ran cold. He stepped toward the window and away from Eve, not wanting to frighten her unnecessarily. "Do you think . . . ?"

"I don't know what to think, Trent," Luke said. "Nothing about this case makes sense, but we can't afford to dismiss the possibility that the Roadside Stalker is targeting Eve."

Trent struggled to fit the pieces together. "There's no way that hair was planted." No one but the people working the case knew about the hair they'd found in Samantha's car. They'd searched every DNA database around without result.

"You're right. It couldn't have been. There's no way anyone could have known whose hair to plant."

Which meant that the criminal targeting Eve, whether the Stalker or someone else, had stepped up his attacks.

"My people are all in place," Luke assured him. "Between them and your video surveillance, I doubt he'll try anything at the house."

Trent sure hoped Luke was right, but the perp had proven himself ruthless.

"As soon as I have anything on the phone tracing, I'll get in touch." Luke ended the call.

Trent stood with his phone still in his hand, staring out at the dreary day.

In the window's reflection, he saw Eve waiting.

He thought he'd finally compartmentalized his feelings for Eve. He'd unpack them from time to time when the past came back to haunt him, but he'd gotten good at stuffing them down deep and simply existing. Getting through each day. Doing what was necessary. But now that he was spending time with her again—and her life was in danger—well, those feelings seemed to have a will of their own. They refused to be suppressed any longer. Maybe it was for the best. Maybe they could get it all out in the open once and for all so he could move on. Still, no matter what, he couldn't let his feelings get in the way of protecting her. She was too important to him.

When he found her watching him, every single thing he'd just promised himself flew out the window.

"Is it bad?" she asked, her voice unsteady.

Trent crossed to where she stood by the fireplace, warming her hands by the dying fire.

"I don't know what it is." He added a few more logs and stirred the flames.

"But Luke had news," she prompted. She'd seen his reaction.

"Yes, he did. They found a hair in your car. Eve, it matches the one from the serial killer Luke and I were tracking together before I left the force."

All the color left her face.

He took her hands. "We don't know anything for certain." It was a lame attempt to reassure her of something he didn't believe.

"But why would that hair be in my car unless he was there?"

He couldn't answer. "I'm going to cancel the work conference call I had —"

She stopped him. "No, Trent. Take your call. I'll be fine. I'll stay inside the house. There are officers nearby, right?"

"There are. Make sure the doors stay locked and keep Jacob close. As soon as the call is over, I'll come back."

"I hate this," she said. "I can't stay a prisoner inside this house forever. I came here to do a job. My grandmother needs my help."

And the sooner Eve finished helping, the sooner she would be gone from his life again.

"I know. I can go with you to do the job." He glanced out at the falling rain. "Until this storm passes, can you focus on taking photos inside? We can try to do outside photos later today."

She straightened her shoulders. "Yes. I need to get with my grandmother and see what she wants to keep. She said something about letting some of the furniture stay with the house."

Trent scanned the familiar room. He couldn't imagine this place belonging to another family. The Lourdeses' family history went back several hundred years. The house had stood as it was since the fire.

"Walk me to the door," he said. Though there were many things left to discuss between them, he hoped they were slowly getting back to where they'd been before that fateful night.

He stopped at the door and faced her. "I'll give you a call when I'm heading back here. Remember what I said about staying inside. Please?"

Trent waited until she'd confirmed before he opened the door and stepped out into the damp morning.

Eve closed the door behind him, and he heard the locks engage with a decisive *click*.

Trent was heading for the SUV when something near the garages caught his eye. He was sure he'd seen movement by the one where Eve had been injured in the explosion. Was it Blake?

Trent reached for his weapon. The memory of Eve being shot at in the woods was too fresh in his mind to let him assume anything was innocent.

Blake's motorcycle had been parked near the front of the house earlier. It was gone.

He eased toward a structure that was set off from the house, where Eve's father used to keep his car.

The roll-up door was closed. Samuel kept a classic car he was restoring inside. But Samuel was gone.

Trent stopped and listened. No sound could be heard coming from inside. Had it been his imagination? He studied the ground and saw fresh footprints. Someone had been here recently. He knelt to examine them. They didn't appear to match the ones he'd seen in the woods and probably belonged to Samuel. Still, he couldn't let it go.

Trent moved to the back and twisted the doorknob. The garage was pitch black inside. He flipped on the lights. Nothing appeared out of place. Samuel's expensive, collectible muscle car sat in its normal place. He went over to the car and tried to open the door but it was locked. He smiled, unsurprised. The car was Samuel's pride and joy.

Trent switched out the lights and left. He'd have to hurry to get back to the cabin and bring up the documents he needed to discuss with his client. Then he'd gather some clothes and ask Jane to let him stay at the house until they could catch the person trying to harm Eve. Even the cabin was too far away when she was in danger.

Trent climbed into the SUV, still bothered. He couldn't dismiss it outright, but all the same, he hadn't gotten a clear look. It was possible it had been an animal, like a squirrel or a rabbit or something. There were plenty of those around.

He drove the short distance to the cabin. As he slid the key into the lock, he glanced through the window and froze.

The back door was open. From what he could see through the window, the place had been ransacked. Whoever had been interrupted before must have come back for a more thorough search. And they wanted something in particular. They had probably watched him and Eve leave and taken the opportunity.

Inside his small office, the desk drawers had been pried open. There was no doubt in Trent's mind that someone had been searching for something in particular. The financial documents Alfred gave him came to mind. It was possible the break-in was a strange coincidence and completely unrelated to what was happening to Eve, but his gut told him otherwise. He'd missed something in the documents that would lead him to the identity of a cold-blooded killer.

Trent grabbed his phone, remembering his conference call. He texted his client and let them know he wouldn't make the meeting, then called Luke.

As soon as Luke answered, Trent said, "Someone broke into the cabin again while I was taking Eve home."

"What could they be after?" Luke sounded as surprised as Trent.

"Maybe the documents Alfred gave me."

"We went over those documents together," Luke said. "I know Alfred thought there was something important in the papers his son-in-law left in his office, but there's nothing we can substantiate other than the original missing funds that Samuel found in Henry's account, which implicated him as the thief."

That was the strange part. The amount of money supposedly missing at that time wasn't even close to the hundreds of thousands the documents showed. Alfred had gone so far as to fire Eve's father when he discovered the missing money in Henry's account, without hearing his son-in-law's side. Trent wondered if Henry had continued to investigate the missing money and discovered something amiss—something apparent in the documents he'd left in Alfred's office.

"I'm going to poke around in Alfred's office," Trent said. "Maybe he missed something significant." Because so far all they had were two financial reports from the Lourdes logging company for the same time period that showed vastly different numbers—a quarter of a million dollars different—plus a faded series number and a name Henry had written on the back of one of the reports, *Kaeman*.

"If he did, and the person who broke into the cabin knows you have the documents, they must believe there's something in there that could incriminate them," Luke said. "Still, I don't understand what any of this has to do with Eve."

Trent didn't either. "They're connected." He didn't know how yet, but there was no doubt in his mind that they were.

"How does any of this fit in with our serial killer? Considering the way Eve was run off the road and the hair found in her SUV, we can't rule out that this could be related to the Stalker case."

"Yeah, you're right," Trent said reluctantly.

Luke was quiet for a moment longer. "Unfortunately, I have some bad news on trying to identify Eve's unknown caller. The number appears to have come from a burner phone. There's no way to trace it."

Trent ran a hand across his forehead. "So we're back to square one, and we still have no idea whether we're dealing with a serial killer hunting his next victim, or someone from Eve's past trying to cover up a crime."

"Exactly. Keep her close, Trent. I'll increase our presence outside the property. Anything else going on?"

"Maybe I'm paranoid at this point, but I thought I saw something by the garages earlier. No one was there when I went to check it out, but I did find some fresh footprints." They might have been left by Samuel earlier, but he doubted it. The rain had washed away all the previous footprints from Eve's attack. "Maybe Jacob went out earlier. Or maybe I imagined seeing the movement."

Luke issued a grim laugh. "Well, if you did, I can certainly understand why after being shot at twice last night and then the attack this morning. Still, until we have a better idea of what's going on, trust your gut. It might save you."

9

$\mathcal{E}$ve paced restlessly by the fire. She wasn't sure which possibility frightened her the most—that some unknown murderer had her in his sights, or that someone from her past was trying to kill her.

Against Eve's will, she thought about her father. In the days following the explosion, he'd been hiding something, according to her mother. When Melanie told Eve that he was leaving, her world fell apart. Was he hiding his involvement in the explosion? Her heart immediately rejected the idea. Even though she hadn't spoken to her dad since she'd been brought into the hospital, she couldn't accept that he would have been involved in anything dangerous. He might not have wanted to be part of her life anymore, but he wouldn't want to harm her.

Would he?

Eve stepped from the living room and headed down the hall to the kitchen. She needed her grandmother more than ever. As she passed Grandpa Alfred's office, she peeked inside and saw her grandfather's old desk. A fractured memory flashed through her mind. An argument. She closed her eyes and tried to pull the memory out. Her father's voice. He'd sounded so angry. There was obviously someone else with him.

Eve rubbed her forehead as if to try and force the memory free, but all she could hear was a muffled voice. Who was the person with her father, and why had they been arguing?

Could it have been her grandfather?

"Eve?"

Her eyes flew open, and she whirled in time to see her grandmother coming her way.

"What is it, child? You look like you've seen a ghost."

Eve flinched at the innocent words.

Gran glanced into the open office. "Have you remembered something from that night?"

Eve dragged in a breath. "I'm not sure. I remember my father arguing with someone in Grandpa's office." She shook her head.

Gran placed her arm around Eve's shoulders. "Honey, you know your dad and Alfred had their differences. It was probably just a disagreement over the handling of some business transaction."

Eve hoped she was right.

"Come and sit." Gran led her to the sofa in the office.

They sat together in silence for a long moment. Eve leaned her head against her grandmother's shoulder as she had when something was bothering her as a child.

"This is all so terrible," Gran murmured. "Does Trent have any idea what's going on yet?"

Eve straightened and faced her grandmother. She hated to burden the sweet woman with what she knew, but if it was connected to a serial killer, everyone between him and his victim was in danger.

She told her grandmother about the possibility that the Roadside Killer was involved, and the threatening phone call she'd received.

Her grandmother gasped. "I remember that case. But there hasn't been a new murder in two years. We all thought it was finally over. Why would he start up again now?"

Eve couldn't begin to understand such evil. "Trent and Luke aren't completely convinced that this is connected to that case. There are some similarities, but there are differences as well." She hesitated. "Do you remember what happened the night of the explosion?"

She'd always believed there were details her family hadn't shared.

Gran's eyes widened. "Of course I remember. It was such a horrible thing. Your poor friend. If you hadn't been a few steps behind her, we would have lost you too."

Though Christy's body had been found inside the garage and the roll-up door was open, Eve had been discovered unconscious behind the garage. Eve had no idea why she'd been back there.

Her grandmother's brilliant blue eyes latched onto hers. "Tell me you're not thinking that the craziness now has anything to do with that. Honey, awful as it was, that was an accident. Whatever is going on now, Trent and Luke will figure out. You're safe here, with your uncles and Trent close and the police officers nearby."

Safe was the last thing Eve felt.

"I hope you will stay awhile," her grandmother said as if seeing a need to flee in her granddaughter's expression. "I've missed you so much. Thank you for agreeing to help with the sale."

Eve smiled. "Of course. Trent is coming over soon. We'll take a stroll around the place and I'll get some photos."

Sadness clouded Gran's expression. "I know this is my decision, but I had no idea how hard it would be to let go of the past. Our past. This has been the Lourdeses' home for generations."

Eve hugged her close. "I can't imagine. Even though I haven't lived here for years, Lourdes Mansion is always the place I think of when I think of home."

Gran gave her a melancholy smile. "I suppose you and I should be discussing the things that will stay with the house when it sells." Her grandmother glanced around the room that represented her husband in every detail. She frowned suddenly. "Although I should tell you, your grandfather's will is missing."

Eve frowned. "Missing? Isn't it on file at his attorney's office?"

Her grandmother shook her head. "No, at least not the updated version. Alfred told me he'd changed his will a few weeks before his death, and that he did obtain signatures from two witnesses, as required by the state, though he didn't say who they were. I asked him to explain the changes, but he wouldn't say anything other than that the alterations would protect you and me."

A shiver ran through Eve. Why did Grandpa Alfred think she and Gran needed protecting? "That's a strange thing to say. And kind of eerie in light of current events. You don't have any idea what he changed?"

"He wouldn't give any details. He was acting very mysterious in those weeks prior to his death. I'd never seen him so spooked."

What had been so troubling to her grandfather that it made him want to alter the will he'd had in place for years? "He never mentioned what was wrong with the original version?" It was out of character for her grandfather. Usually, if something were troubling him, he wasn't shy about expressing his thoughts.

"No, never. I tried to question him more—ask him why he needed these changes—but he told me the less I knew, the better." Gran shook her head. "He was always such a straightforward man that I thought this was odd, but Alfred had a good head on his shoulders and I trusted him completely, so I didn't question it. He would never act impulsively." Gran's voice caught, and Eve reached for her hand.

"Do you think he left it somewhere here in his office and never got around to giving it to his attorney?"

Gran's eyes darkened. "We checked in his desk and the file cabinet. There was nothing."

Eve rose. "Where else could it be?" Her attention landed on the bookcase. She headed over to it and began flipping through the books. "Can you think of any place else he might keep it?"

"No. He rarely went into the office at the real estate development firm anymore, but I had Samuel search his desk there. No luck."

Why would Grandpa Alfred want to change the will so suddenly? He loved his children equally.

Eve finished searching the books on the shelves and went over to the desk. She stopped when she realized the bronze statue of a soldier riding a magnificent horse was missing.

Eve pivoted toward her grandmother. "Where's Grandpa Alfred's statue?" For as long as she could remember, that statue had been on her grandfather's desk. She'd sit on her grandfather's lap while he was talking on the phone and simply gaze at the enchanting sculpture, memorizing its lines and curves.

Gran frowned and moved to the desk. "I don't know. I haven't been able to come in here much since his death. I had Jacob search for the will." Her eyes held tears. "I don't know why Alfred would have moved the statue. It was one of his favorites." She scanned the room. "There are several other pieces missing as well." She pointed to the file cabinet. "He loved collecting western statues. There was another bronze there, and over on that wall, he had a signed landscape piece. It was appraised at around a hundred thousand dollars."

And the bronze pieces had been designed by a famous American West sculptor. Was it possible someone had come into the house and taken them?

"Who else has been in the house, besides family?" Eve asked her grandmother.

Gran realized what Eve was asking. "No one who would steal from us."

Her grandmother had a big heart, and she always saw the best in everyone. Still, there was no denying someone had moved or taken the objects.

"Maybe we should put off going around the property until later." Eve's brows knitted together. First her grandfather's will and now some of his treasured pieces were missing. She didn't like it.

Gran clasped her hand. "No, honey. You go ahead. Trent will make sure you're safe."

Eve wasn't concerned about her own safety at the moment. Had her grandmother unknowingly allowed a killer into her presence? How else would someone have gotten into the house and removed the items?

Could it even have been someone her grandmother knew and trusted completely?

She'd have to let Trent know what she suspected. "All right." Eve glanced at the time on her phone. "I should probably change before we head out. Are you sure you're okay?"

Gran smiled a little sadly. "I'm fine."

Eve reached the door, but her grandmother remained in the middle of the room. "Are you coming?" Eve asked.

"No, I think I'll stay in here for a while. I've missed this room. It makes me feel closer to him."

Eve's heart went out to her grieving grandmother. She and Grandpa Alfred had been together for more than fifty years. Gran had told her many times that she and her husband had genuinely enjoyed each other's company so much that it didn't matter what they were doing, as long as they were together.

Eve watched her grandmother sink into her late husband's chair and thought about the future she'd once hoped for with Trent. Seeing him again had proven there was still a strong attraction. Was it possible she could still have the future she'd once dreamed of with him?

She closed the door and started for the stairs. She met her aunt Renee coming from the kitchen.

When she spotted Eve, Renee stopped and placed her hands

on her hips. "What are you doing in my father's office? Hoping for something to steal?" The words struck like blows. Renee wore a nasty smile as she continued. "Are you here to fleece the family like your money-hungry father?"

Eve didn't understand the animosity her aunt held for her. Renee had never really had much time for her niece when Eve was a child, but there hadn't been any outright hostility.

And after discovering that pieces were missing from Grandpa Alfred's study, Eve thought it was interesting that Renee had accused her—and her father—of stealing. She lifted her chin. "What are you talking about? Why would you say that about my father?"

Renee sneered. "Maybe you should ask your mother. I'm sure she knows. After all, she married him. Or better yet, why don't you go back to Syracuse before something bad happens?" Renee pushed past Eve and headed upstairs.

Eve watched her leave with a sense of dread. While she had no idea what Renee was talking about, Eve had always believed there was more behind why her father left his job with the Lourdeses' logging company—and his own wife and daughter—than what she'd been told. Was that what Renee had been referring to when she mentioned Eve's "money-hungry father"?

The entire encounter left Eve shaken. Hoping to avoid another run-in with her aunt, Eve grabbed her camera, along with the weapon Trent had given her, and headed outside. Though Trent had asked her not to leave the house without him, she desperately needed to clear her head and she was skilled in using a handgun.

She closed the door and a sudden feeling of unease swamped her. She forced it down. Trent would be back any moment and there were police officers close. No one in their right mind would attempt to harm her with so much police presence.

Goosebumps peppered Eve's arms as she stepped from the porch. She would be cautious and take a few pictures around the grounds while she waited.

Since she'd gotten her real estate license, Eve had found that she enjoyed taking photographs. It was relaxing, and she had begun doing it as a hobby as well as for work. It gave her a chance to get out into nature, to capture and highlight tiny miracles that would otherwise go unnoticed. She'd taken many photos around Syracuse, and she and her mother often drove to the small towns around upper New York to take snapshots.

Eve slung the camera strap over her neck and started toward the stables. As she neared the rebuilt garage, her footsteps faltered. Suddenly, she was back in that long-ago night when she'd been getting ready to take Christy home.

Eve rubbed her temples. Every time she tried to remember something about the night of the explosion, she ended up with a migraine. She stopped suddenly to catch her breath. Why had she and Christy come to the rebuilt garage when the multicar garage housing her old Volkswagen bug was on the other side?

She focused hard on the emerging memory. A flat tire. Her car had a flat tire. It had been losing air for a while, and her father had warned her to get it changed, but she hadn't, so she'd needed to borrow his car to take Christy home. She'd gone to get her father's keys from him when she'd heard an argument and stopped. Whomever her father had been arguing with—the conversation had been fierce.

Eve had remembered her father kept a spare set of keys on the workbench in the garage. She and Christy had started in that direction and—

She couldn't bring it out. She balled her hands into fists as the memory dissolved.

Eve closed her eyes again to try to hold onto it.

The roll-up door had opened but she hadn't gone inside. Something had distracted her behind the garage, and she'd gone to check. Christy went inside. What had distracted Eve? Try as she might, she couldn't grasp the rest of the memory.

"What are you doing?"

Eve suppressed a scream and, weapon in hand, whirled toward the voice.

Jacob held up his hands. "Whoa, Evie. I'm sorry. I didn't mean to startle you. Can you put that away?"

"I'm so sorry." Eve struggled to regulate her pulse. She stuffed the weapon back into her jacket pocket.

Jacob reached her side. "No harm done. Are you okay?"

She drew in several cleansing breaths. "I think I'm beginning to recover my missing memories." She told him what she'd recalled so far. "My father was having a heated conversation with someone, but I can't seem to remember who it was."

"Evie, that's great. What do you think your father and this mystery person were arguing about?"

Eve shook her head. "I have no idea, but whatever it was, they were really angry."

"It could be nothing," Jacob said gently. "You know how your father and mine liked to argue. They were probably having one of their usual disagreements."

Maybe, but Eve didn't think so. There had been something different about her father's tone.

"Why are you out here, anyway? You know Trent told you to stay inside," her uncle chided. "Not that you can't handle yourself with that gun."

She told him about her encounter with Renee. "I don't understand why she hates me."

Jacob chuckled and put his arm around her shoulders. "She doesn't hate you—or at least not only you. Renee dislikes everyone. Don't let her get to you. She enjoys getting people riled up." He pointed to her camera. "Are you starting on the photos outside? Want me to tag along?"

She appreciated the offer, but he'd clearly been on his way to work. "No, I'll be fine. Trent's coming over."

"You sure?"

"I'm sure," she said as firmly as she could manage. "I wouldn't want to make you late for work."

He cringed. "Yeah, working with my brother is a real drag. Even though I handle most of the business, he still checks up on me. I'll see you later." He waved and headed toward the multicar garage.

She watched him go, reflecting that she had pulled a gun on a member of her family. Being close to the site of the explosion had rattled her. She needed to get away.

The noise of the river that ran through the property gave her an idea. Eve texted Trent to meet her and headed toward the sound.

As she walked, she heard Jacob's vehicle leaving through the gates.

Because of the recent rain, she found that the river ran swiftly and was close to overflowing its bank. Eve gingerly picked her way down to the water's edge to get the full effect of its beauty.

She clicked several photos, smiling at the happy memories the scene brought back. Summertime was her favorite season. She and Trent would go down to the river to swim, usually along with Luke and Christy. Sometimes Jacob would join them as well.

She'd treasured those lazy days with Trent. She'd been so in love with him. She couldn't wait for their next moments together. When it was just the two of them, they'd spread a blanket out and sit side by side, talking for hours, stealing little kisses and holding hands. Their young love had seemed like it would never end.

But it had. And she'd been the one to end it. After losing Christy, she'd been so bewildered and distraught. Then her father had walked out on Eve and her mother when they needed him the most. Then, on top of losing Christy and her dad, there was the feeling that something terrifying waited for her at Lourdes Estate. She'd known she couldn't return there without digging up painful memories. So, where had that left her and Trent?

Eve struggled to let go of the past. She and Trent weren't the same two people anymore. It wasn't as if they could simply pick up where they'd left off. She stepped closer to the riverbank, leaning in close to capture the breathtaking foliage across the water.

A twig snapped. A dark figure appeared in her peripheral vision.

"Sorry, I thought I'd go ahead and start," she said, assuming it was Trent.

Someone shoved her hard.

She screamed and fought to keep her footing, to no avail.

She hit the frigid, raging water, and it knocked the breath from her body.

Her limbs froze, and her face slipped below the surface.

10

"Help!"

Trent whirled toward the sound of Eve's terrified screams with his phone still up to his ear. The call he'd received moments before ended abruptly, and a text message from Eve came through. *Meet me at the river.*

Her calls for help came from that direction. She'd gone out without him despite his cautioning.

"Hold on!" he yelled, hoping she could hear him. He charged toward the river, arms pumping at his sides. His heart pounded out a rhythm—*no, no, no.*

Trent shoved branches out of his way as the noise of the river grew louder. Eve's screams were barely audible.

He reached the bank and searched the water for her. "Eve, where are you?"

"Over here. Hurry, Trent. I can't hold on much longer."

He focused on the spot, several hundred feet down from his location. The water was littered with debris from upstream. She'd managed to catch a downed tree limb, but she was clearly fighting to stay afloat.

"I'm coming!" He pushed through the heavy foliage along the edge of the water until he got ahead of her location. Trent seized a tender young tree branch and bent it down so it stretched across the water. "Grab this, Eve."

The very top of the branch was just out of her reach. She'd have to swim to it.

"I can't reach it." The desperation on her face was terrifying. She was a strong person and an even stronger swimmer, but the current was too much even for her.

"Yes, you can. You can, Eve. But you're going to have to let go of the log."

She shook her head rapidly. "The water is moving too fast. I can't fight it."

"You can do it. It's not that far. Remember that summer when I fell in and you saved me? Trust me."

Eve held his gaze and released the log. She focused her attention on the limb and began swimming toward it.

Trent's pulse pounded in his ears in time with each stroke. His heart ticked off every second.

She strained to reach the limb and wrapped her fingers around it. "I've got it!"

Relief flooded his body. "Hang on and pull yourself toward me."

Using the branch as a guideline, Eve worked her way to shore, hand over hand. Finally, she stood in the shallows.

Trent let go of the tree and waded to her. He wrapped his arms around her and guided her from the water. "Let's get you back to the house."

She was shivering uncontrollably. "No. I don't want my grandmother to see me like this. Can we go back to your cabin instead?"

"Sure." He led her away from the river. "What happened? Why were you out here by yourself?" Now that he knew she was safe, he was irritated that she'd gone out alone against his warnings, but it was all his fault she'd almost died.

He'd received a call shortly before he was to meet Eve. Trent didn't recognize the number, and there was no one on the other end when he'd answered. He'd fallen for one of the most basic tricks he knew of. Someone had purposefully delayed him in order to harm Eve.

"Someone pushed me into the water," she said through chattering teeth.

Trent stopped suddenly. "What?" How had they gotten past the guards? The one route he could think of was the gap in the wall where the river cut through the grounds.

Eve told him about the figure she'd seen nearby. "I thought it was you, but then they shoved me so that I fell in."

Trent glanced around, expecting another attack at any moment. "Let's get out of the open. You need to change out of those wet clothes and warm up."

He ushered her into the cabin and locked the door. Trent grabbed a towel from the linen closet and wrapped it around her shoulders. He went to his room and found a set of sweats that would be way too big for her, but they were the best he could do.

"Here you go. There's a hair dryer in the bathroom. If you want to take a hot shower, feel free."

She smiled gratefully. "Thanks, that sounds nice. I'll be back."

Eve closed the door behind her.

Trent stacked wood into the woodstove along with kindling, then lit the fire. Once it was burning, he grabbed his phone from his back pocket and brought up the number that had called him. He hit redial, but the call went unanswered.

Trent listened to the shower running and rubbed a hand over his eyes. He didn't doubt for a moment that the call was meant to distract him from meeting Eve.

He called Luke and filled him in.

"It's disturbing that he got past my officers. They're stationed all along the property line," Luke said.

"The estate is huge," Trent said. "I guess it's possible the perp could have entered from a different point, or near the river. Hang on."

He pulled up the video feed showing different parts of the property. He hadn't put a camera near the water because the river was too hard to cross, so the attack on Eve hadn't been captured.

"I got nothing on any of my video feeds," Trent said into the phone. How had the person gotten across the river?

Down the hall, the shower water shut off.

"He's smart," Luke responded. "He found a way to cross the river without being detected. How is Eve holding up? I imagine she's having a tough time, with what she's been through these last couple of days."

"She's scared to death, but you know Eve. She keeps pushing through. I'm going to stay at the house with her and the family."

"Good idea. We have four officers stationed around the house, but I'll add more to be safe."

Trent blew out a sigh. "Thanks, Luke."

"Was anything missing after this last break-in?" Luke asked.

In the next room, the hair dryer clicked on, pulling Trent's attention away for a second.

"No, and I did a thorough search." It made no sense. "Anything on the car or the fingerprints you took from the cabin?"

"Nothing," Luke said. "There are dozens of cars that match the description Eve gave. Without a license plate number, we may not be able to locate the car, and we weren't able to match the fingerprints to anyone on file."

Trent ran a hand through his hair, his frustration growing with each dead end they ran into. Alfred's fear for his granddaughter was at the forefront of his mind. Eve's grandfather had suspected someone might eventually target her. "I haven't had the chance to search Alfred's office or revisit the bank statements he gave me."

"Alfred was convinced Eve's father left those documents in his office, but he also thought Henry was the one embezzling from the firm," Luke mused. "How did Alfred even know for certain that Henry printed them himself? Someone else could have gone into his office and printed them." His skepticism was clear.

"True, but Alfred seemed pretty convinced it was Henry who left the documents in his office. He believed Henry planned to come back for them, but Henry left after the explosion."

"For what purpose?" Luke asked. "He'd already been fired for stealing from the business. Why print statements that would confirm his guilt?"

"Unless they don't. The numbers on one document indicate that the amount of funds missing is far different from what Samuel found." Trent thought about the scribbled series of numbers on the back of one of the bank statements, and the name *Kaeman* with a question mark. What did they mean? Who was Kaeman? Trent was still trying to figure out their significance.

Alfred had been convinced that the real reason Henry left was because he feared he'd be thrown in jail, until Alfred had found the documents. Trent had known Henry for years. He was a decent man, and Eve adored her father. Everyone had been shocked when Alfred fired his son-in-law for allegedly stealing from the company.

"I think Henry was on the verge of figuring out who really took the money when everything fell apart."

"It's possible, I guess," Luke said, still sounding unconvinced. "Who had access to the financials back then?"

"To my knowledge, it was Henry and Alfred, Samuel, and the accountant, Lawrence Jenkins."

"Where's Jenkins now?"

A good question. Trent had been trying to locate the man for a couple of weeks. "He left the business after Alfred's death and hasn't responded to my recent attempts to contact him."

"Really? Maybe he's the one who took the money, and he set up Henry to take the fall," Luke said.

"Or it could be something innocent. We need to talk to Jenkins."

"You want me to see if I can locate him?"

"Please." So far, Trent had more questions than answers. He glanced over his shoulder as the hair dryer shut off. "That'd be great. I've got to go. Eve doesn't know any of this yet. Especially the part about her father being fired."

"You've got to tell her, Trent. She has the right to know that the recent attacks might be connected to the missing funds."

He hated betraying Alfred's confidence, but in light of the assault at the river, he was beginning to wonder if someone from within the family might be responsible. If so, Eve needed to know so she could be on her guard. He thought about Renee's ex, Blake, who had once worked for the logging business. According to Alfred, Henry was the only one besides Renee who could get along with Blake.

"You're right, she does," Trent agreed.

"Before I go, I do have a piece of strange news. We were able to identify the tracks left by the car as those of a small sedan."

The one witness to the Stalker's crimes had claimed he'd seen a dark sedan on the same road where one of their victims had later been forced off.

"Still," Luke continued, "we don't know whether those murders have anything to do with what's happening to Eve."

Trent rolled his shoulders to relieve the stress. "I don't think I can buy that this is a simple coincidence."

"Neither can I, and I did some checking. Guess who has a small sedan registered in their name?"

Trent froze in place. "Who?"

"Blake Wilkins."

"Blake? He's ridden a motorcycle for as long as I can remember." The thought of the Stalker being so close all along was terrifying. Especially with Eve back home. "What do we know about Blake's whereabouts during the murders? If I remember correctly, he and Renee weren't together when the Stalker was active."

"Probably not," Luke said. "They've been on and off for years. We searched the records back then and his name didn't come up. I think he was living in California. I guess he came home again and registered the car here in New York. A lucky break for us."

"Not the smartest move, if he is the Stalker," Trent observed. "I don't like the guy, but besides his ability to manipulate Renee and mooch off her family, I never would have thought of him as a killer."

"Agreed. Still, he has to be investigated. His vehicle matches the description of the car that ran Eve off the road, as well as the one our witness claimed to have seen, which might belong to the Stalker. And it matches the one you reported hanging out around the property. I know Blake's been at the family estate a lot lately, but he does have a small house in town. We're going to see if we can catch up with him there. Maybe check out the car and see if we can pull DNA."

"Let me know what he has to say."

"I will. In the meantime, watch your backs," Luke warned. "There are a lot of unknowns right now. If Blake is trying to hurt Eve, we don't have enough to bring him in yet. He could be back at the estate soon. And whether or not Blake is related to the past murders, there's a chance he and Renee could be up to something. Keep your eyes on them."

"I will. We'll talk soon." He ended the call as Eve stepped from the bathroom. Seeing her wearing his old academy sweats made him smile. Even in gray sweats, she'd never been more beautiful.

"How are you feeling?" he asked when he realized he was staring.

"Much better. At least I've stopped shivering." She held up her wet clothes. "Do you mind if I toss these in the dryer?"

He pointed her in the right direction and she left the room.

While he had her alone, it was a good time to tell Eve about her grandfather's suspicions.

He went over to stoke the fire before adding some logs. The dampness of the day seemed to penetrate the house and seep into his bones.

Eve came into the room and settled in one of the rockers in front of the fire's warmth. "Any news?"

Trent claimed the rocker beside her. "Not really. Luke is stationing more officers around the house."

She leaned her head back against the rocker. "I can't shake the feeling this is all somehow connected to the explosion. I don't think it was an accident, Trent. Someone was trying to silence my father, but it didn't work."

And Christy had died because of it. Alfred had hinted as much himself.

"Back then, no one expected a motive behind the explosion," Trent said. "The police assumed the chemicals that were stored there had been ignited by the faulty wiring. But before his death, your grandfather seemed to think the explosion wasn't an accident."

Her eyes widened. "But why would someone do such a thing?"

Until he fully understood what the documents meant, he didn't have a clear answer for her. "I'm not sure."

Eve sat up straighter. "I had a run-in with Renee before I left the house." She told him about her aunt's accusations.

Trent considered what he knew of Renee. She'd been adopted by Alfred and Jane as an infant and raised as one of their own. Though Renee wasn't working, at one time, she'd been employed in the office of the Lourdeses' logging business. She could have found a way to access the bank accounts and withdraw the missing money.

"She's always been distant with me, but since I've been home this time, she seems to actively dislike me," Eve said.

It was strange. Perhaps Renee didn't think Eve or her mother deserved to be part of the benefits of the business because they'd moved away. Or maybe she wanted it all for herself.

"Do you think it's because of Grandpa's updated will? It's missing."

The new piece of information didn't sit well. "We need to find that will. Maybe it will clear things up." Trent hesitated for just a second, but it was enough for her to notice.

"What's wrong?"

"Luke was able to pull tire imprints from what seems to be a small sedan, which would match your description. The thing is, the Roadside Stalker was thought to drive a car fitting that description." Shockwaves of fear rolled across her face as he told her about Blake owning such a car.

She covered her mouth in surprise. "Do you think Blake is capable of murder?"

Trent wouldn't have believed it before. "I'm not sure." He was struggling to see Blake as a serial killer. Yet even if Blake wasn't connected to the murder cases, Trent remembered that he and Renee were still married at the time of the explosion and Blake had worked at the family's logging mill along with Henry. If Blake and Renee had taken the money, then they certainly wouldn't want Henry exposing their crimes. And if the explosion had been set up to take out Henry, then Eve might have seen something.

Her brain had blocked out certain memories from that time. If Eve had seen the person who set the explosion—Blake or Renee or both—and her memories returned, they couldn't afford to let her live.

11

Was it possible her own aunt wanted her dead and had reached out to Blake for help?

The dryer buzzed that it was done, and Eve started. Almost drowning had left her on edge.

"Gran must be going out of her mind by now. I've been gone for a long time." Still, being with Trent made her feel safe and she didn't want to leave. She hadn't felt that way in years.

"Sounds like your clothes are dry. Are you ready to head back?" Trent asked when she didn't move.

She shook her head. "Not yet." She simply wanted to stay in that safe place with him for a little while longer. "You think someone took Grandpa Alfred's will because they didn't like what was in it?"

"I'd say that's a good possibility," Trent said, watching her expression. "What is it?"

"I want to ask you something." Eve gathered her courage. "Can you tell me what you know about my father's leaving? He never explained it to me, and Mom said very little about it other than he didn't want to be married to her anymore. She was so crushed that I didn't have the heart to push her for answers." She searched Trent's face. "But the thing is, he and my mother always seemed so in love, even though Grandpa Alfred thought my dad married my mom for the money."

The sympathy in Trent's eyes made asking that much harder.

"I don't know why your father left, Eve," he said gently. "I spoke to Alfred about it many times, and he was furious with Henry until—"

He stopped. Something bad was coming. How much more could she take?

"Until?" she prompted when he remained silent. "Tell me, Trent."

"A large amount of money went missing from your family's company right before the explosion. Alfred was certain your father had taken it. In fact, he fired Henry when the funds went missing. Alfred suspected that was the real reason your father left—he was afraid of being arrested."

So that was what Renee had meant when she accused Eve of stealing like her father. "Why would he do such a thing?" Her dad, a criminal? She couldn't wrap her head around it. "Grandpa Alfred might not have liked my father, but he would have given him anything he needed. There was no need to steal from the business."

Trent searched her face. "Well, that's just it. Alfred changed his mind about your father's guilt before he died." He told her about the documents that were found in Alfred's office. "Henry was investigating the missing funds and discovered it was a far greater amount than originally thought. The real thief was determined not to be exposed and willing to do anything to protect themselves, including set off an explosion that was meant to take down Henry."

Eve's mouth dropped open. "Dad was trying to reveal the truth. But why would he leave if he was innocent?"

Trent clasped her hands in his. "Whatever the reason was, he loved you and Melanie. Very much."

The father she'd known back then had loved Eve and her mother dearly. There was no doubt in her mind about it. She'd experienced that love in everything he did for them.

An emotional exhaustion like she hadn't felt in years bore down, and all she wanted to do was return to her quiet life in Syracuse and forget about her father and the nightmare that had welcomed her to her childhood home. Eve pulled her hands free and rose. "I should get my clothes. I'd like to get the photos taken as soon as possible so that I can go home."

Trent stood as well. "That's not a good idea, Eve. Someone is targeting you. Whether this is related to what happened twelve years ago or to the Roadside Stalker, it won't matter if you're here or in Syracuse. You're in danger either way."

She put space between them. "I promised my grandmother I would help her out and I won't let her down. But as soon as I'm finished, I'm leaving."

"Eve." The sorrow in his eyes was painful to witness. He lifted his palms in a gesture of resignation. "I can't stop you from leaving, I guess, but I'm coming with you on the photo shoot."

The strong set of his jaw reminded her of times past when they'd had minor disagreements. Despite the emotions flaring between them, the memories made her smile. "All right. I'll go change. I dropped my camera by the water's edge and I need to go back for it. I hope it's okay."

She had a backup camera, but the one she'd dropped was her favorite. Eve left the room to put on her dry clothes and when she came out, Trent was on the phone again.

"I updated Luke on what we're doing," he said once he ended the call.

She could imagine Luke's stern disapproval.

"He's put more officers up near the house and around the property. It should be safe enough."

They stepped out into a different world from earlier. The sun was trying to break free of the clouds, and thankfully the rain had stopped.

"Why don't we take the horses," Trent suggested. "They'll be better able to traverse some of the rough terrain on the property."

Eve hadn't been on the back of a horse since she'd left home, and the idea was appealing. At one time, she'd loved to ride with her father, her uncles, and her grandfather.

"I'd like that," she told him softly. "We could pack a lunch since it's bound to take a while." Visions of the many times she and Trent had ridden horses and picnicked in the past crowded in. She'd loved every minute of their time together. Eve's life had been somewhat solitary since she and her mother had left. Physically, she'd healed from the trauma of the explosion and from losing her friend, but she had always been sure there was something waiting in the shadows of her missing memories, ready to destroy any amount of happiness she'd manage to achieve.

She'd attended a local university and thrown herself into her work. She was happy. At least that's what she told herself. But she'd missed her life here and always wondered what would have been if the explosion had never taken place—an explosion that might not have been an accident after all, but rather an attempt to silence her father.

When she and Trent found her camera, Eve did a careful examination. "I don't think it's damaged," she said in relief. "I'll clean it up and it should be fine."

They passed several police officers as they neared the house. Having them close eased some of her concern. She couldn't imagine the attacker trying to hurt her again with their increased presence.

She and Trent stepped up onto the porch.

"I'll get the horses saddled and meet you out front," Trent told her.

She nodded and watched him head toward the stables, stopping briefly to speak with one of the officers. A part of her would always love him. They'd meant so much to each other once, until she'd destroyed everything because she'd been afraid to stick around, afraid her mind would unveil a truth she couldn't deal with. Something more had happened the night of the explosion. At times, she could almost feel it waiting in the dark recesses of her mind, ready to drag her away. She'd been running from it for years, but she couldn't run anymore.

Eve slipped inside the quiet house and tried to release the sadness in her heart.

The last thing she wanted was another conversation with Renee when she was feeling so vulnerable. Especially with the idea that her aunt might be trying to kill her.

Both Samuel and Jacob were at work. She stepped into the kitchen and found Betsy stirring something on the stove that smelled delicious.

Betsy faced her with a smile. "Well, there you are. Jane said you were up and about. Would you and Trent like some lunch? It would be nice for the four of us to catch up." Betsy's smile faltered. "Is something wrong?"

Betsy had been nothing but kind, and Eve didn't believe she was in any way connected to the threats on her life.

Eve forced a smile. "No, nothing. Can I have a rain check on the chat? I want to take some photos around the place."

Betsy laid down her spoon and wiped her hands on her apron. "Of course." She glanced around the room. "It must be hard being back after . . ." She didn't finish and appeared embarrassed to bring up the past. "I can't even imagine this place not belonging to the Lourdes."

Eve felt the same way. "Neither can I. There are so many good memories here."

Betsy swept her golden-brown hair out of her face, her deep blue eyes filled with sympathy. "I know, honey." She gathered Eve close. "I know."

Eve was barely hanging on emotionally. Getting through her time alone with Trent was going to be hard enough. She couldn't fall apart or she'd never be able to get herself back together. "I'd better hurry," she said, and untangled herself from Betsy's grasp.

"I'm making a picnic lunch for myself and Trent. He's coming with me on the photo shoot."

Something shifted in Betsy's eyes. "You two were always so good together." She didn't say anything more, but Eve knew that like so many others, Betsy didn't understand why she'd fled Lourdes Mansion. Why she'd let Trent go.

"I'll help you prep your picnic." Betsy went to the pantry and brought out some bread. "There's chicken salad in the refrigerator, and fresh fruit."

Eve opened the fridge and pulled out the food.

She and Betsy talked while they worked. It was nice to spend time with her aunt.

Once the picnic basket was packed, Eve's phone alerted her to a text message. "It's Trent. He's outside."

Betsy handed her the basket. "You go ahead, hon, but be careful."

Eve hugged her once more, grabbed a blanket from the hall closet, and stepped out into the clearer weather.

Trent watched her as she approached. Eve could feel her cheeks grow warm under his attention. Did he see it? She hoped not. Things were going to be hard enough as it was without him knowing how she still felt about him.

He took the basket from her.

Eve stroked the muzzle of the mare she'd be riding before easing into the saddle. Unlike Uncle Samuel's Arabian show horses, these two mares were gentle quarter horses trained for riding.

Eve nudged the mare's flanks with her heels and started off at a slow trot with Trent by her side. They would start the photo shoot in the pasture behind the house.

She could almost feel Trent's tension. He continually scanned their surroundings as she snapped several photos to show the vastness of the estate.

"I'd forgotten how beautiful this place is," she said when they stopped for lunch. Though she'd been away for years and had been reluctant to return, the estate was starting to feel like home again. Eve was grateful for the chance to say goodbye.

Trent held the basket while she spread the blanket on the ground, then settled next to her on the soft fabric.

"We've had some good times here," he said, glancing around the pretty meadow she'd chosen for their picnic. Soon it would be covered in wildflowers.

"We have," Eve agreed as she unpacked the food and handed him a sandwich.

Trent was as much a part of this land as she was. The more time she spent with him, the more she realized she was still in love with him. That scared her. She'd barely survived having to leave him before. How could she get through it again?

Her life was no longer here, and once the family home sold, her last tie to the area would be gone. Where did that leave them? They couldn't go back to the people they'd been before that horrible night.

"What's bothering you?" he asked, setting down his sandwich.

She couldn't tell him that her heart was breaking.

Eve wiped her hands on her napkin. "I was thinking about all the lovely memories I have of this place. Everywhere I look, I see my grandfather. All the times he and I used to ride all over this property. Or the Easter egg hunt we'd have in the south valley. The Christmas scavenger hunts he put together. Grandpa Alfred used to hide our presents around the place and give us little clues where to find them. He was so much fun, and I miss him a lot." Tears burned the back of her eyes. "It's going to be hard letting it go—letting *him* go."

He held her gaze for a long moment. "Almost like letting go of a piece of yourself."

"Exactly." Eve couldn't break the eye contact. She didn't want to. Once she left, she might never come back here again. Never see Trent again. If she were being honest, he was as much a part of her good memories as her grandparents.

"You remember the time we decided to hunt for gold?" she asked, grinning. "You, me, Luke, and Christy. We'd watched some show on TV and were convinced there was gold everywhere."

Trent chuckled. "I remember how mad your grandfather was when he discovered all the holes we'd dug."

She laughed as well. "He made us fill them all in."

Trent made a face. "It wasn't nearly as much fun covering them as it was digging."

"That's because you had it in your head we were going to be filthy rich gold miners." She shook her head. "There was no talking you out of it."

"And you were all in," he asserted. "You were so cute with your face covered in dirt, digging for gold." Trent leaned closer and brushed a crumb from her cheek, and suddenly she wasn't smiling anymore. His fingers lingered on her skin. His expression was the same one he'd worn before he'd kissed her for the first time.

Her heart thrashed against her chest. She couldn't do this. Not again. It wouldn't be fair to him when she had no plans to stay.

Eve stumbled to her feet, her breathing hard and labored. "We should finish up. The clouds are moving back in."

"Eve." Trent rose and came toward her.

"No." She backed away and he stopped. "Please, Trent. Can we just finish and go?"

The heartbreak in his eyes was yet something else to be sorry for.

"Okay." His voice sounded so empty. Without another word, he gathered the leftovers of their lunch and tossed them into the basket while Eve folded the blanket with hands that shook.

She should never have suggested a picnic.

They mounted their horses and rode to the far side of the property without speaking. It had already been an exhausting day and Eve's heart was as dreary as the gathering clouds.

They stopped at a small ridge on the property where her grandfather used to take her whenever they rode. Eve snapped several photos of the valley below, another place that reminded her so strongly of Grandpa Alfred.

A flash in the distance made her jerk away from the panoramic view. A breath later, the noise of gunshots cracked across the valley.

Her horse whinnied in terror and reared up on its hind legs. The mare bolted, along with Trent's mount.

"Hold on, Eve!" Trent yelled from behind her.

Another round of shots made her press herself down against the mare as they galloped at a frightening speed along the downhill path. When the shooting stopped, she pulled up hard on the reins and struggled before finally bringing the horse to a stop.

Trent caught up with her. "Are you hurt?"

She shook her head no, unable to speak. The wild ride had stolen her breath.

"We need to get out of the open in case the shooter is still out there." He pointed to the nearby woods, and they rode in that direction.

Eve was even more certain now that whatever was hidden in her mind about the night of the explosion, it had someone scared enough to want to commit murder. As much as she wanted to pack up and flee back to her quiet existence in Syracuse, she had to put aside her fear and find out the truth once and for all. She owed it to Christy and to herself to know what had really happened.

12

*H*aving managed to evade gunfire as they swiftly made their way through the woods, Eve and Trent were finally safe indoors, at least for the time being. But even with police officers crawling around the property, Trent couldn't let his guard down for a second. The shots fired had proven he'd made a huge mistake by letting Eve go out in the open to take photos. If she'd been hurt, he would never have forgiven himself.

Shooting at victims wasn't part of the Stalker's MO. While someone might be trying to make them believe everything was related to the killer who had haunted the streets years ago, Trent was convinced the shooter was much closer to Eve.

"It's not your fault." Her voice broke through his unsettled thoughts.

He turned from the window where he'd been staring out at another rainy afternoon, berating himself for not taking more care. "Isn't it?" His mouth twisted wryly. "I'm a former police officer, Eve. I should have seen this coming."

She came over to him, "Trent, there are police officers stationed all around the property. This guy is brazen."

And increasing his attacks. For some reason, the shooter was more and more determined to get Eve out of the picture.

Someone knocked on the door of Alfred's office. Eve started toward it, but Trent stopped her. "Let me." He scanned her weary face. He doubted she'd slept much in the past twenty-four hours. "Why don't you stretch out on the sofa and get some rest?" he suggested. "I'll be close."

She barely let him finish. "No, Trent. This guy is coming after me. I'm not going to cower behind you and the rest of the police force. I want to be part of this. I *am* part of this." She squared her shoulders, clearly prepared to do battle. "The longer this goes on, the more likely it is that he'll hurt someone I love, whether on purpose or not. Like Aunt Betsy or Gran. I can't let that happen."

Though he was terrified of losing her to this criminal, he admired her courage. He opened the door and waited for her to step out into the hallway.

As soon as Trent saw Luke's face, he knew the truth. "He got away."

Luke nodded, his jaw tight with anger. "He may have used a four-wheeler to get onto the property at the far side where we weren't expecting an attack. I'm guessing he had a truck and trailer stashed somewhere. The good news is we found the spot where the shooter was set up. A single set of footprints indicates one shooter. And he was rushed with all the police presence, so he left behind shell casings."

"That's great. What type of weapon did he use?" Eve asked with a hint of anticipation.

"Some type of long-range rifle," Luke told her. "Obviously different from the 9mm used earlier."

"So two different weapons, but the same shooter?" Trent wasn't so sure. If everything was connected to the explosion, then it was also likely connected to the missing funds. The logging business records from twelve years before were probably long gone. Especially if someone within the business was responsible for taking the money. Someone like Blake and Renee.

"Anything you need?" Luke asked, his full attention on Trent.

"I need you to send me the police records from the explosion."

Luke didn't hesitate. "I can get that for you. Until we catch this guy, I've increased the manpower around the property. Two of our neighboring police forces have agreed to assist so that we can have the extra police presence on-site. Still, after today, I can't stress enough the need to be careful."

Trent agreed. "I'd like to show Eve the information Alfred left me. Perhaps something about the name on the back or the number will jog a memory. I'll run out and pick it up from my office."

Eve swung to face Trent, shaking her head. "I'm going with you. I'll feel safer."

Though her answer thrilled him, taking her out into the open again could be dangerous.

Before he could argue the point, Luke's phone buzzed with an incoming message. As he scanned it, all the color left his face. "Oh no."

Trent's heart thundered in his chest. "Something with the case?"

"No. A missing person's report came in. A woman." Luke captured Trent's gaze. "Her parents reported her gone. They expected her hours ago. When she didn't show, they went looking for her at her house."

Trent braced for what he knew was coming. "They found a note."

Luke nodded and the bottom fell out of Trent's world. The Roadside Stalker had returned.

But was he the same person coming after Eve?

"And there's more. We've located her car north of town. There's damage, like the others, and like there was to Eve's SUV. I've got to go. I'll have the police report sent to your phone." He frowned at Eve. "Although I don't recommend you go with Trent, if you insist, I can have some of my officers accompany you both for added protection."

"Thank you, Luke," Eve said.

Trent struggled for calm. "Let me know what you find." He watched Luke hurry from the house while the weight of the devastating news settled on his shoulders. With the Stalker at large, taking Eve out into harm's way seemed foolish. "I really think you should stay here, Eve.

It's too dangerous. I mean, you got back last night, and how many times have you already been attacked?"

She shook her head. "I feel safer with you than I would with a dozen officers standing guard. He's coming after me, Trent," she stressed when he remained silent. "And you're right. This has everything to do with the night of the explosion. I'm tired of living in fear. Waiting for something from the past to pounce. I want to be part of figuring out the truth of the past so it can be laid to rest once and for all."

The risk was tremendous, but he understood what she was saying. Despite everything, he wanted her close, so he nodded in agreement, as a new email notification sounded from his phone. Luke had been true to his word. He'd sent the police report from the night of the explosion.

After enough time had passed for Luke to travel to where the missing woman's vehicle had been abandoned, Trent called Luke to thank him for the report and to let him know they'd be leaving soon. For Eve's benefit, he put the call on speaker. "Do you know anything about the victim yet?" Trent asked.

"I just arrived at the scene where the car went off the road out near the Blevins property. It's scary how well it matches what happened to Eve's vehicle." Luke paused for a long moment. "Anyway, as soon as I know anything, I'll call. In the meantime—"

"Be careful," Trent finished for him.

Two officers waited outside, and Trent spoke to them briefly as he and Eve stepped out the door. "It might be safer to use different transportation that the perp won't be familiar with." Alfred's old four-wheel-drive vehicle was still stored in one of the garages. He and the older man had taken a few trips up to the mountains in it to go hunting before Alfred had died.

Once he and Eve were one their way, the police cruiser slipped into place behind them.

"Do you still go to the mountains?" Eve asked as they headed for Winter Lake. "My grandfather told me the two of you used to go hunting."

Trent smiled despite the tension that had burrowed into his shoulders. His heart warmed at the knowledge that she remembered how much he'd enjoyed spending time in the mountains growing up, whether simply connecting with nature or hunting. He felt the most alive there. "I do, although I haven't in a while. It's harder to get away these days."

Trent remembered all the times he and Eve would head to the mountains with Luke and sometimes Christy. They'd spend the time four-wheeling up in the high country. So many of his good memories were tied to Eve.

Trent pulled onto the street where his office was located across from the police station. He stopped in front of the building as their police escort pulled up beside them and both officers got out.

"I'll check inside before you go in," one officer said, then went to search the building while the other waited with Eve and Trent. "All's clear," he told them when he came back out.

"Thank you." With Eve at his side, Trent led them into the building.

Eve glanced curiously around his office. "Do you like being your own boss?"

He considered the question for a second. In many ways, he enjoyed the freedom of choosing his own cases, but there would always be a part of him that missed being a police officer. After all, it had been his lifelong dream.

"I guess I do." He kept his answer vague as he moved around to his desk. His safe was mounted into the wall behind a painting of Winter Lake. He punched in the code and opened the door. The safe was empty except for the manila envelope containing the two financial documents.

Eve slipped into the chair across from him.

"How about we start with the police report from the night of the explosion and see if it brings anything new to the surface?" Trent sat at his computer and opened the email Luke had sent earlier.

Eve pulled her chair around beside him—as always, it was a struggle to stay focused with her close.

According to the report, the family's gardener at the time stated that he never stored chemical fertilizer in the single-car garage. The wiring connected to that garage door opener had been replaced within the past few years and should not have been faulty, and Henry's car was the only one parked in the garage at the time. In Trent's mind, Henry must have been the intended target. So why was someone trying to silence Eve if not for something she'd witnessed that night—something they knew would incriminate them?

"So, the police never thought the explosion was anything but an accident, despite our gardener's statement?" Eve asked.

He scanned the rest of the report, but there was no record of anyone else admitting to placing the chemicals in the garage. Trent sat back in his seat. "Apparently." Given the family's clout in the area, the police had written the incident off as a tragic accident, even though Christy had died.

The rest of the report yielded nothing useful. He opened the envelope containing the two documents Alfred had given him and spread them out beside each other.

Eve scooted forward and stared at the pages before blowing out a breath. "I have no idea what I'm looking at here."

He smiled. "I had to have your grandfather explain it to me." He explained the differences between the two reports and pointed to the bogus one. "Someone had been taking money from the logging mill at the time, and they created two separate reports, one legit and the other doctored. These were found in Alfred's office, but the money was first discovered when the accountant became suspicious."

She frowned.

"The money apparently never made it into the business bank account. Some customers paid in cash. Others by check. Apparently, the checks were cashed, but we're not sure what happened to the money. I'm guessing some was deposited, but we don't know what percentage exactly."

"Or by whom?"

"Exactly. As I said, the scope of the theft wasn't clear in the beginning. The accountant contacted Alfred because the numbers from the month of the explosion seemed lower than usual. Alfred did some digging and discovered your father was in charge of gathering the checks that month. Several thousand dollars had gone missing and were deposited in Henry's account. Alfred blamed your father and fired him."

Eve shook her head. "He never gave him a chance to explain?"

"No," Trent said quietly. "Something he later regretted." He pointed to the two documents. "These reports are different from the one that raised the accountant's suspicions. They go back several years before the time of the explosion."

"Meaning someone had been stealing money for years."

"Exactly. And hiding it well. Alfred was certain Henry was investigating the discrepancies and the person who was actually taking the money got scared. They had to do something to throw off suspicion."

"The real thief managed to get my father fired. And when Dad still didn't let it go, the thief was willing to kill to cover up his crimes." Eve's hand covered her mouth. "Poor Christy. It's my fault that she's dead."

"No, Eve," he said, taking her hands in his. "None of this is your fault."

She swallowed several times. "Isn't it? I was going to take my father's car that night because I hadn't gotten the flat tire on mine repaired." Eve pulled her hands free, flipped the documents over, and scowled. "Wait, what is this?" She'd noticed the numbers on the back, along with the name.

"We're not sure of the significance."

"Kaeman." She repeated the name several times before swiveling her chair to face him. "I remember hearing my father saying 'Kaeman' the night of the accident." She told him about the argument she'd overheard.

"As in the Cayman Islands?" Trent slapped his forehead. "It's not a name, it's a location. Henry must have misspelled the word so no one else would guess. I can't believe I didn't see this before. The stolen money was parked in an account in the Cayman Islands." He pointed to the corresponding number beside the name. "That is probably the bank account."

"We need to find out whose account that is," Eve said.

But it wouldn't be easy to get information on an international account.

She dropped the paper and rose to pace the office. "So what does any of this have to do with me?"

He lifted his shoulders. "It's simple, Eve. You must have seen something that can identify the person who set the explosion. The person probably responsible for taking the money."

A noise from the storage room outside the office grabbed his attention and Trent jumped to his feet.

Eve must have heard it too. Her huge round eyes were fixed on him.

"Stay here and lock the door." Trent drew his gun and headed past her toward the opening.

When he reached it, a figure jumped out from behind the door and slammed something hard against the back of his head. He dropped to his knees and the image blurred before his eyes. Another blow took him to a world of darkness.

13

Too paralyzed with fear to scream, Eve watched in horror as Trent slumped to the ground.

The figure whirled toward her. He was dressed in black, his face hidden under a ski mask, eyes covered with sunglasses.

"No, please!" she cried out as he stalked toward her.

His hand snaked around her throat, cutting off her air supply.

Eve fought with all her strength. She clawed at the hand around her neck, tried to pry it free, but he was far too strong for her and she could feel herself losing consciousness. The dark image faded before her eyes. *Not like this.*

The man suddenly jerked his head toward the door as if he'd heard something. He flung Eve away from him. She flew across the room and slammed into the wall, then slid to the floor. The man scooped up the documents from Trent's desk and headed for the door. He stepped over Trent's lifeless body as if he were nothing, and then he was gone.

Eve tried to scream but near strangulation made it difficult to even speak. She scrambled over to Trent, terrified she'd lost him. She pressed her fingers to his throat and nearly wept with relief when she felt a pulse. "Trent? Can you hear me?" Eve shook him and his eyes opened. "I'll get help," she croaked. She ran to the front of the building and waved desperately to the officers outside. Luke was there with them, and they all came charging toward her.

Without waiting to explain, Eve ran back to Trent and gathered him in her arms. "Help is coming. Don't try to move." She couldn't stop shaking. They'd both almost died, and the key evidence in the case was gone. She had no doubt whoever took the money would have erased all digital evidence of it, and getting a bank in the Caymans to give them details on the account would be a legal nightmare. They had nothing to identify the killer breathing down their necks.

Luke and the rest of his team raced into the office. Luke immediately ordered the officer at his side to call an ambulance, then knelt to examine his friend's wounds.

Trent winced and pushed his hand away. "I'm okay. What happened?"

Eve struggled to get the words out. "He hit you with something and knocked you out." Her voice was hoarse, and speaking was painful. "Then he grabbed the documents and went out the back door."

Luke motioned to the officers, who headed in the direction she'd indicated.

"Did he say anything to you?" Luke asked.

Eve shook her head. He hadn't, but there had been something familiar about him. How did she know him?

The two officers returned. "There's no sign of him," one said. "We didn't see him enter the building or hear a vehicle leaving, so I'm guessing he found a way to sneak in, and had a getaway car stashed somewhere."

Luke radioed for extra man power to search the surrounding area and the two officers left to assist. Then he helped Trent up and walked him over to one of the chairs.

"I'm okay, really." Trent held his head and closed his eyes. "Quit fussing."

"You are anything but fine," Luke said drily. "Eve, is there anything you can tell me about the man that might help us figure out who he is?"

She started to shake her head and then stopped. There *was* something. "He was a little more than average height, probably close to yours and Trent's, with a slender build. I couldn't see his hair—he wore a ski mask over his head." She told him about the sunglasses. The build of the person who'd attacked her could match any number of people she knew, including Blake.

"Did anyone else know you were coming here today?" Luke asked them both.

Eve shook her head again.

"I didn't tell anyone either," Trent said. "We think we've figured out what the name and number on the back of the one report means, though." Trent told him about the Cayman Islands theory.

"Great. Do you remember the number?" Luke asked.

Trent's disappointment was clear. "I don't. So we have nothing."

"We'll figure it out," Luke said grimly. "Once the EMTs have checked you out, I'll have my officers follow you back to the house."

Trent nodded and then grabbed his head. The movement must have been painful. "How will we figure it out? They have the evidence Alfred gave me."

"They were worried it could point to them." Luke rubbed his jaw thoughtfully.

"You said my grandfather found the documents in his office?" Eve interjected. "I wonder if there might have been other evidence left there." She and Gran had searched the room for the missing will without success, but then again, they weren't trying to find anything but the missing will. "I think we should go back there and take another look around."

She told Luke and Trent about the missing art pieces. "My grandmother told me she hadn't been in the office since my grandfather passed away. She doesn't know when the pieces might have gone missing."

Trent frowned. "They could be totally unconnected to the document theft, but we have to try everything. Let's do a thorough search when we get back to the mansion." Trent's gaze shifted to Luke.

"What about the missing woman?"

"We have a team searching for her now," Luke told them. "We don't know anything for certain, but the pattern does fit the Roadside Stalker's previous behavior."

"That poor girl." Eve couldn't imagine what she'd gone through. She prayed Luke's people would find her before it was too late.

"Where's the killer been?" Trent asked the question on Eve's mind. "Samantha was his last known victim and I've checked all the national databases. There have been no other reported murders matching these."

Luke shook his head. "We went to Blake's house. He wasn't home and there was no sign of the car."

Blake had always been strange and gave Eve the creeps, but was he a killer? "Was he even here at the time of the murders?"

"He was," Luke confirmed. "And I did some checking around for any crimes like our case. About ten years ago there was a string of attacks on young women that could have been the killer working his way up to murder."

Luke saw their surprised expressions and added, "The attacks took place one county over—where Blake was originally from. There were a total of five young women who reported that someone tried to grab them."

"Unbelievable," Eve said. "And you think Blake might be the person who committed those crimes and the murders?"

"It's possible," Luke said. "Think about it. He and Renee were together when the killings took place here, and then he disappeared. The killings stopped. He was around at the time of the other attacks."

"And now he's back and he's staying at the house," Eve said with a shuddering sigh. "That makes me sick to my stomach."

"We don't know for certain Blake is connected to any of the crimes yet," Luke warned. "And the missing person might prove to be unrelated."

Outside, the ambulance siren wailed. Its mournful sound shivered down Eve's frame, closing in on their location like the killer who had her in his crosshairs.

14

Jake Templeton, the lead paramedic, examined Trent's head injury gently, then sat back on his haunches. "Any blurred or double vision?"

Trent shook his head and winced. "Nothing but a nasty headache."

Jake grinned. "I can give you something for that. First, let me get the wound cleaned and bandaged. You've had a tough few days." He indicated Trent's previous injuries.

While Jake worked, Trent watched Eve. She'd almost died at the hands of their unknown assailant, who had been so determined to get to her that he'd risked capture by officers standing right outside the building, right across from the police department.

"There you go," Jake said. "If you do experience any of the symptoms we discussed, you need to get to the hospital right away. Understood?"

"I will, I promise," Trent said and managed to smile though Jake appeared skeptical. Probably because he and Trent had gone through school together and played on the same football team. He knew Trent well.

"Here, take two of these." He handed Trent a bottle of tablets. "They'll help with the headache. Don't take more than two in a four-hour period." Jake gave him some water.

Trent opened the bottle and swallowed two, then took a sip to wash them down. "I won't. Thanks, Jake."

Jake closed his bag and went to assist his partner, who was caring for Eve.

Luke sat down beside Trent. "How's the head?"

"Not great. How's she doing?" Trent nodded toward Eve.

"She's shaken up." Luke didn't mince words. "This keeps getting worse, Trent. Stay glued to her side."

The uncertainty in Luke's tone catapulted Trent's apprehension into overdrive. "Any word on the missing person case yet?"

Luke shook his head. "I'm going to be pulled in as lead, but I'll still continue working Eve's case, of course."

"What about Blake? You have to bring him in for questioning."

"We will. I have an all-points bulletin out on his car, his bike, and Blake himself," Luke answered. "There's been no sign of him around the estate. And I've had my team question Renee."

"What did she say?"

"She denies any involvement in what is happening with Eve, and she was clearly shocked by the possible connection between Blake and the car we believe belongs to the Roadside Stalker."

Still, Trent didn't trust Renee at all. "She has been openly hostile toward Eve. I'm not so sure she's blameless. Maybe she's simply a good actress."

"That's why I'm glad you'll be there with Eve, and Jacob and Samuel as well, in case Renee is involved. Obviously, Blake won't be allowed back on the property, and Renee knows this."

The EMT finished Eve's exam, and Luke rose. "Get her home. She's been through enough. CSI will comb the office as well as the surrounding area to see if we can find any trace evidence left behind."

"Thanks, Luke." Trent went over to Eve, who was unsteady on her feet. "Let's get you home." He gathered her close and they left the building with Luke and the two officers who were to accompany them.

"Call me if anything out of the ordinary comes up on the trip home," Luke commanded. "And be safe."

Trent nodded and held the door open for Eve, then helped her into the vehicle. Once she was inside, he scanned the surrounding area before getting in.

As soon as they'd pulled onto the main road, their police escort fell in behind them. Having a police presence gave Trent only a small amount of comfort. The person coming after Eve was desperate. And desperate people did deadly things.

"What is it?" Eve glanced over her shoulder.

"Nothing," he assured her. "Just making sure our escort is close." He reached for her hand. "Try to relax." It was on the tip of his tongue to tell her she was safe but he couldn't lie to Eve, and safety was something he couldn't guarantee at the moment.

When they were about halfway back to the estate, the skies opened up. Trent slowed the vehicle under the torrent of rain. He could feel Eve's tension growing.

Trent switched on his lights as the rain made the afternoon appear almost as dark as night. Up ahead, a vehicle approached some distance away. He gripped the wheel tight as they hit a waterlogged spot on the road, causing brief hydroplaning.

Eve sucked in a breath while he fought to get the vehicle under control again.

The lights of the upcoming car grew brighter. Trent squinted as it passed them. He couldn't see the driver, but the car sent goosebumps down his arms.

A small dark-colored sedan.

"Is that him?" Eve craned her neck to follow the car's progress.

"I don't know." Trent grabbed his phone and called the officers behind them.

"We see it and we're going after it now," the officer said. "Are you and Eve okay by yourselves?"

Trent glanced at Eve, whose face was pale with terror. "We'll be okay," he said, as much to reassure her as the officers.

Lights flashing, the police cruiser pulled a U-turn and went after the car.

Trent's heart rate pounded crazily as he kept his attention on the road ahead, periodically checking the rearview mirror. The car appeared to pull over without incident. The flashing lights descended on it.

"He's not putting up a fight," Eve said in a doubtful tone.

"No, he isn't. We don't know for certain that it's Blake or the guy we're chasing."

She slowly relaxed. "You're right. It could be some innocent person caught in the rain who happened to be driving a small sedan."

They reached the entrance to the estate. Seeing patrol vehicles along the Lourdes property line made Trent expel a relieved breath as he steered onto the drive.

His cell phone rang as they pulled up to the gate and punched in the code. "It's Luke." Trent answered and put it on speaker. "What's up?"

"Turns out the man in the car was Blake," Luke replied without preamble. "My people have him in custody. I'm at the station now, waiting for him to arrive. I'll give you a call as soon as we know something."

"Thanks, Luke." Trent ended the call and passed through the gate.

"I still can't believe Blake is the one responsible," Eve said.

He didn't miss the doubt in her voice.

He parked by the mansion, then got out and went around to Eve's door to open it for her. They rushed up the steps and into the house.

Samuel and Betsy appeared from the living room at the sound of their entry.

"Eve, there you are." Samuel headed toward them. "We've been so anxious. Mom told us what you went through earlier. I went out to have a look around the place when we couldn't find you in the house."

Eve hugged her uncle close. "Sorry, Uncle Samuel. We should have told you we had to go into Trent's office. But we're okay."

Samuel held her a little away from him. "Has something else happened?"

Eve relayed the attack at Trent's office in town.

Samuel gaped at her. "That's awful, Evie. I'm wondering if it might be safer for you to return to Syracuse until the police can figure all of this out. Melanie must be beside herself."

"I haven't told her yet. I didn't want to worry her."

Jacob and Jane came out from the kitchen. Jane raced toward them, examining the marks on Eve's throat. "What's going on?"

"Let's go into the living room," Trent said, his concern for her growing.

Eve sank down into the chair nearest the fire while Trent caught everyone up. He noticed that Renee was nowhere around. "The police have taken Blake into custody," he concluded.

A ripple of shock ran through the group.

"Blake? I don't understand," Jacob said. "What does Blake have to do with the attacks on Eve?" His gaze moved between Trent and Eve.

"We don't know anything yet," Trent answered.

Jane took Eve's hand and helped her stand. "Honey, you must be exhausted. Come and have something to eat with the family. We were about to have dinner. And then you should get some rest." Jane patted Trent's arm as they passed him. "I'm so glad you're here with her. I've made up the room next to Eve's so you'll be nearby in case of danger."

Trent smiled. "Thank you, Jane."

Eve walked beside her grandmother like someone in a trance. He'd seen the same expression many times while working with victims of crimes. It took a while for the truth to sink in.

In the dining room, Trent claimed the chair beside Eve while

Betsy and Jane placed bowls of soup on the table and the rest of the family filed in.

"I thought with the chill in the air, my mother's hearty beef stew would be fitting." Jane squeezed Eve's arm and sat down on the other side of her. "And Betsy made her rustic bread."

"It smells delicious," Trent said.

Eve remained silent, staring at her food.

Trent broke the silence by asking, "Jane, where's Renee this evening?"

"She wasn't feeling well." Jane frowned. "But now that you've mentioned Blake, I wonder if he might be the reason she isn't feeling well. I never understood what she saw in him to make her keep taking him back." Jane shook her head. "I'll take something to eat up to her room once we've finished."

"Trent, what do you think the attacker was after at your office?" Samuel asked. "Did he follow you there to hurt Eve, or is there another reason?"

Trent set down his spoon. Alfred had chosen not to share the details of the documents with his family for a reason, and Trent would honor that—especially since he no longer knew whom he could trust. "We're not sure. It was a pretty brazen move though, with the police department right there."

Samuel shook his head. "No kidding."

"I got here a couple of hours ago. I haven't noticed anything unusual," Jacob told them. "But I heard on the news that a woman has gone missing outside of town. Do you think what happened to Eve is related to Roadside Stalker?"

Beside him, Trent saw Eve flinch.

"We don't know anything for certain yet," Trent assured him, briefly clasping Eve's hand.

"Well, we're here to help in any way you need, Trent," Jacob told him. "I, for one, won't be able to rest until this is all sorted out and my favorite niece is safe and sound."

Since Eve was his only niece, the joke usually made her laugh, but it was almost as if she hadn't heard it.

Once the meal was over, Trent waited for Eve outside the dining room. "You really should try and get some rest," he told her.

She shook her head. "I'm far too keyed up to sleep. I'd like to take another look around Grandpa Alfred's office."

Trent readily agreed. "Let's take our coffee with us." He opened the door to the office and waited for Eve to go in ahead of him. He closed the door and watched her stop in the middle of the room.

"I'm not sure where else to search. Gran and I gave the room a pretty thorough going-over," Eve told him.

He surveyed the room. "You mentioned that your grandfather is missing some art?"

"Yes." Her shoulders slumped in defeat. He hated what this was doing to her. "The bronze piece my grandfather kept on his desk. The picture, and another statue."

So someone had been pilfering from the estate as well. What else had gone missing? "Did Jane report the theft?"

Eve shook her head. "No, she said she didn't want to bother the police in case they turn up, but I think she's afraid someone from the family might be responsible."

He was positive of it. A theory began to form in his mind. "What if someone in the family found out about the documents Alfred gave me to investigate—such as the person responsible for taking the money from the business?" Was it Renee? He wanted to know about her finances. He'd see if Luke could run them for him.

The expression on Eve's face scared him. "Are you okay?" he asked, regretting the words as soon as they were out of his mouth.

She appeared to have lost all color. "No. The night of the explosion. I told you I heard my father arguing with someone. It wasn't my grandfather. But the voice—it was familiar."

"Was it a woman?"

"I don't think so." She closed her eyes and fisted her hand against her forehead. "I'd give anything to remember."

His heart went out to her. No matter what, he'd always love her and want what was best for her. He pressed her arm, and she opened her eyes.

"Your memories will come back, Eve," he said gently. "I know you haven't wanted to return here, but I think it's going to be the thing that gives you back those missing pieces."

Studying her face transported him back in time. He stepped closer, almost afraid to breathe and risk breaking the spell.

Tears hovered in her eyes. She cupped his face with her hand and pressed her lips to his. Her kiss was the same as it had been before she'd left, and yet everything had changed. She wasn't his any longer. And he couldn't go through the pain of losing her again if he opened up his heart once more.

Trent kissed her back, then reluctantly let her go and stepped away. He'd made a promise to Alfred to keep her safe, but he would have done that even if Alfred hadn't asked, because he still cared. He reflected that it was interesting that he would do anything to protect her because he couldn't protect his heart from her.

He cleared his throat. "If a member of the family saw Alfred meeting with me, they might have guessed it had something to do with the missing funds. They might have even found the changed will. And if I were able to track down who took the money, they'd know it was only a matter of time before we discovered the explosion that killed Christy wasn't an accident. Whoever is responsible is facing murder charges on top of everything else."

"They'd certainly want to silence me if I could identify them." Eve bit her lip as she thought. "The night of the explosion, there was a noise behind the garage. Someone was there." Her eyes widened as they locked with his.

"The person had to act fast. They were trying to get rid of Henry. They never expected it to be you and Christy," Trent said.

And an innocent woman had died.

"Wait. I remember something from before the accident. When my father was arguing with someone. He got a call on his cell phone in the middle of it."

"Really? Do you remember what happened next?"

"I do. My father stepped from the room and passed by me as if he didn't see me. He waited until he was out of earshot to take the call."

"What about the other person? Did he come out of the room?" He knew he was being pushy, but they were so close. If she could remember the person Henry had argued with, they might have the identity of Christy's murderer and the one who was trying to kill Eve now.

"No, but I didn't stay that long. I went downstairs to where Christy was waiting."

Trent struggled to put the rest of the pieces together. "So you and Christy headed to the garage where your car was parked?"

Eve hesitated for a moment before she shook her head. "It wasn't in the garage. Christy and I had used it earlier, but the tire had a slow leak. I didn't want to drive it any farther, so I'd parked it out front. I wasn't able to speak to my father because of that phone call I mentioned, but I knew he kept a spare set of keys in the garage, so Christy and I were on our way to grab those."

"Where was your mother at the time?"

Eve didn't hesitate. "With Betsy. She and Betsy had gone to the movies."

That had been confirmed by both women, as well as by the movie attendant on duty, according to the police report.

"Okay, so you were heading for your father's garage." After Henry got the phone call, there may have been enough time for whoever was in that room with him to slip into the garage and put the finishing touches on a pre-planned explosion. But why would they think Henry would be using his car that night—unless the call had been a ploy, possibly to lure Henry to the garage. If that were the case, then there had to be more than one person involved in the act.

It had to be at least a pair—like Renee and Blake.

15

"I'm going to step outside and call Luke to see if he's found anything on Blake or the missing woman yet."

Eve nodded because words wouldn't come. She was emotionally emptied, as much by Trent's pushing her away after she'd kissed him as by the realization that someone from her family might be trying to kill her to cover up past crimes.

"I'll be right outside." Trent left the room and closed the door.

As much as she wished she could believe Blake and Renee were responsible for the attempts on her life and for the explosion, she didn't.

She could hear Trent's quiet voice in the hallway. Tears filled her eyes. She still loved him. Why hadn't she trusted him to be there for her, to help keep her safe?

Eve scrubbed the tears aside. Had it really been just over twenty-four hours since she'd arrived back home and stepped right into a nightmare? She hadn't spoken to her mother in hours—Mom had to be wondering what was going on.

Eve retrieved her cell phone and called her.

"There you are," Melanie answered. "I've been trying to reach you for a while but the calls kept going to voice mail. I know service can be sketchy around the estate."

Her mother's voice, full of love and concern in such a terrifying time, nearly undid her. Eve tried to steady her voice enough to speak.

"Honey? Is something wrong?"

Her mother had the right to know what was happening. Eve pulled in a breath and told her everything. "Did Daddy ever mention having problems at the logging business? Specifically, missing money from the account?"

"No, never. Oh, honey, you need to come home. Now. I was afraid it would be too much for you, but I never imagined someone from the family would want to hurt you. If this is Renee's and Blake's doing, who knows what criminals they might have hired to help them?"

Eve chose her words carefully. "Mom, I can't. I have to see this through. Besides, Trent is here with me, as are Jacob and Samuel, and Luke has officers stationed all around the property. I'm as safe as I can be. Besides, if I come home now, it won't change anything. It might even bring danger to your door, and I don't want that."

"This is all so unbelievable," her mother said sadly. "And all for money. I always got the sense that Renee felt she didn't belong because she was adopted, but that wasn't because of anything our parents did. They loved her. *We* loved her."

Eve's mother had told her Renee's parents, close family friends, died in a car accident. Jane and Alfred couldn't let Renee go into foster care, so they'd brought the two-year-old home and loved her as their own.

"Did you know that Grandpa Alfred fired Daddy?"

"What? No. Who told you this?"

"Trent told me Grandpa Alfred mentioned it. He said he was fired when the money went missing. Some of it was found in Daddy's private account."

Her mother was silent for a long time. "My father never mentioned any of this to me."

"He probably didn't want to upset you."

"I'm coming. I can be there by morning. I won't let you go through this alone."

Eve couldn't let her mother put herself in danger. "No, Mom, it's too dangerous. Promise me you won't."

The door opened and Trent returned.

Seeing him—knowing how she'd messed things up between them—hurt so much.

"Look, Mom, I have to go, but I'll call you back, I promise. As soon as I have more news."

Her mother hesitated for a long time before she spoke again. "Okay, honey, but you stay safe. I can't lose you too." There was a catch in her voice that reminded Eve of all the things her mom had lost.

"You won't. I promise." Eve ended the call and faced Trent. "Has there been any news?" She hated that her voice wasn't steady.

"They are still speaking with Blake, and two of the officers have taken Renee in for further questioning as well."

Her eyes widened. "So Luke believes Blake and Renee are responsible?"

Trent came further into the room, and she fought to keep from backing away. Why was she suddenly so jumpy around him? Maybe because that kiss had reminded her how much she still cared for him—and his withdrawal afterward had reminded her that she'd blown it for good.

"Not necessarily. But they can't rule them out completely. Blake was out on the road. He said he was driving around to find some good places to take photos, but that could just be a cover. He could have easily parked behind the office and come in through the back door to attack us. It would have given him plenty of time to get to where we saw him on the road."

"What about Renee? How does she fit into this?" Eve asked.

"We're not sure yet. She's being questioned on Blake's whereabouts of late. Luke wants to see if what she says matches Blake's statement because he's using Renee as his alibi for both the time of the attack today and the time the young woman went missing."

Outside, lightning flashed across the sky. A few seconds later, thunder rumbled the windows and shook the doors.

"Sounds like we're in for another round of storms," Trent added, not quite able to keep the edge from his tone. He walked over to the window and pulled the curtains shut.

Together, they combed through the office without any luck. There was no new information and no will.

"Do you think my grandfather kept the most recent version of his will somewhere else?" As far as Eve knew, before his death, he rarely went into the office. Had someone found the will and destroyed it?

Trent was quiet for a bit, thinking. "I don't think so."

So they had no idea where the latest will was, and she couldn't help but suspect that her father had found something which would incriminate the person stealing money from the Lourdeses' company—something her grandfather hadn't known about.

"You should try and get some sleep," he said gently. "Did you get any rest last night?"

Eve lifted her shoulders. "Not really."

"Come on. We're not having any luck here." He took her hand. "Let's try to catch a few hours' sleep. I think we have a long road ahead of us before we have answers."

They were headed toward the stairs when the front door burst open. Eve whirled around as Renee stormed into the house.

Trent tugged Eve close to his side.

Renee spotted them and stopped. The anger inside her seemed to radiate all around. "This is all your fault," she hissed. "Because of you, Blake is being treated like a criminal."

Jacob and Samuel stepped from the living room, followed close by Gran and Betsy.

"This isn't Eve's fault, Renee," Jacob told his sister. "She's the victim here."

"She's not a victim," Renee snapped. "She's the reason all of this is happening."

Eve leaned against Trent, who held her tighter.

"I'm going to stay in town. I won't be part of a family that accuses me and the man I love of such dreadful things." She started for the stairs.

"Renee, wait," her mother called after her. "Let's talk about this."

Renee ignored her. She hurried up the stairs and, a second later, a door slammed.

"Well, that didn't go well," Jacob said, going over to where Eve and Trent stood. "I'm sorry, Evie. Don't let Renee upset you. She's foolish to defend Blake. Hopefully, she'll see that in time. He's always been a bad apple, and we'll make sure he doesn't come back here."

"Thank you, Jacob," Eve said. "I'm going to try to get some rest."

Jacob looked at her with sympathy. "That's a good idea. You'll feel better once you've slept."

She didn't want to risk another run-in with Renee, but she didn't have to worry for long. Moments later, Renee stomped back down the stairs with her suitcase and left the house without another word.

Why did her aunt have so much hatred toward her? Was it because Renee was the one responsible for the explosion and knew that at some point Eve might remember the truth?

Eve said good night to the rest of the family, and she and Trent started up the stairs. As much as she'd love to have this nightmare over with, her gut wouldn't let her believe Blake was capable of such violence, even if the anger she'd seen in Renee certainly felt directed at Eve.

"If you'd asked me if I thought Blake was capable of such a thing a week ago, I would have said no. Now nothing makes sense and everyone is a suspect," Trent told her.

She shivered as she thought about someone close wanting her dead. Why would they? She didn't know anything about what her father had discovered. He hadn't left her any clues that would help fit the pieces together, and she didn't remember anything that would point to the guilty party.

Trent stopped in front of her door. "Try not to worry. I'm right next door if you need anything."

Eve studied his handsome face, and felt her heart crack. If she survived this, where would it leave her and Trent?

She ran the back of her hand along the side of his face. "Thank you, Trent. For protecting me." She swallowed, but the lump in her throat wouldn't go away. "It's more than I expected after the way I ended things between us. You deserved so much better, and for that I'm sorry."

A muscle worked in his jaw. "Get some rest," he said with an edge to his tone. He walked past her to the next room. Without another glance, he went into the room and quietly closed the door.

Eve bit back a sob. Tears blurred her vision and she fumbled to open her own door. She closed it and leaned back against it while the tears ran freely.

Outside her childhood room, the storm hit with a downpour of rain and a lightning show that was truly frightening. As if even the weather was foretelling a showdown that had been twelve years in the making.

Since remembering the argument between her father and someone else, more pieces of the past had begun to resurface. The night of the explosion, she'd seen a mysterious figure fleeing from near the back of the garage. His stance had been familiar. She knew him—knew Christy's killer. Was it Blake? As hard as she tried to recall further details, she couldn't.

Eve flipped on the lights and headed across the room to close the curtains. Having them open made her feel exposed. She was halfway there when the lights suddenly went out. The storm had taken out the power, and the ensuing darkness felt like a living presence, pressing in around her. It was too much. She ran from the room.

Before she could call out for Trent, someone grabbed hold of her and a hand clamped over her mouth. The person yanked her toward the landing, as if to push her down the stairs.

Eve stamped hard on her attacker's foot.

He let out a yelp and loosened his hold, so she shoved him away and ran for her life.

"Trent!" she screamed, sprinting to his room. She had to reach it before the man caught up with her. A person could only escape death so many times, and she knew her number was running out.

16

$\mathcal{E}$ve had screamed his name.

Trent dropped his phone on the bed, dashed across the room, and wrenched open his door.

She spotted him in the darkness and ran into his arms, shaking all over.

"What is it?" He ushered her into his room and locked the door.

"S-someone grabbed me," she stammered. "They tried to throw me down the stairs."

Her attacker was in the house. Trent couldn't let him get away. "Stay here and lock the door behind me. I'm going after him."

"No, Trent, please." She grabbed his arm to keep him there.

Trent covered her hand with his. "I'll be okay. Lock the door."

He retrieved his weapon and flashlight from the dresser and moved out into the hall, then waited for Eve to click the lock in place before he eased toward the stairs to listen. The house was quiet. Where was the rest of the family? Trent searched the rooms on the second floor. Renee's room was in disarray after her hasty departure. Jacob's was empty. Samuel and Betsy's room was on the first floor near Jane's.

He reached the bottom stair. A faint pool of light flooded out from beneath the door of Alfred's office. Trent drew in a breath and jerked it open.

Jacob and Samuel stood near the windows, listening to the radio. Both men looked up as he entered the room.

"What's wrong?" Samuel asked with a frown.

Trent started to ask why they hadn't heard Eve scream, but with the radio and the noise of the storm raging it would have been difficult for them to hear anything.

"Someone attacked Eve and tried to throw her down the stairs." Both men reacted with shock.

"Was she hurt?" Jacob asked, a sharp edge to his tone.

Trent lowered his weapon and light. There were a couple of lanterns scattered around the room. "She's shaken up but unhurt. Did you hear anyone leaving the house?"

"No, we didn't," Samuel told him. "It's terrifying to think that he was in the house and we had no idea. Do you think he's still here?" Samuel's wide eyes conveyed how unnerving the thought was.

"I don't know. Stay here and lock up behind me. I'll clear the house. Where are Betsy and Jane?" Trent asked.

"They both went to bed," Samuel explained. "Mom was pretty upset when Renee left."

Trent nodded and started out the door. "I'll be back. Lock up behind me." After a careful search of the first floor yielded nothing, he went back to the brothers. "There's no sign of the perp. I'm going to check in with the officers outside."

Trent grabbed his rain gear and went out into the storm, which was growing in intensity. Two officers watched the front of the house. He spoke to the closest one. "Did you notice anyone leaving the premises?"

The officer appeared surprised. "Not since Renee earlier. There's been no one in or out."

It didn't make sense. How had Eve's attacker managed to get past the police?

"You want me to check with the other officers and see if they noticed something unusual?"

"Go ahead." Trent waited while the officer called his people. Even before he had verbal confirmation, Trent knew the answer.

"No one saw anything suspicious. We'll search around and see if we can find him."

With the storm's intensity, it might have been possible for the attacker to leave the property without being seen. Still, Trent had doubts.

"Thank you." Trent left the officer and returned to the house, hastily relocking the door behind him.

Jacob and Samuel came out to meet him.

"Where can he be?" Jacob asked.

"It's a big house. Keep your eyes open. If you see or hear anything, let me know. I'm going up to check on Eve."

"I can't believe this," Samuel said. "After everything Evie's been through, it would be a pity if something were to happen to her."

Trent focused on Samuel for a long moment. A strange thing to say, but then, Samuel was always a bit awkward when it came to emotional matters. Someone who didn't know him might think he was arrogant, but Trent knew Samuel well enough to see the truth—he was a quiet man who sometimes struggled to relay his feelings.

"Evie is important to Jacob and me," Samuel added. "She's like our little sister."

Trent clamped his shoulder before grabbing one of the lanterns.

Arriving at Eve's door, he knocked twice. "Eve, it's me." A handful of seconds passed before the lock released and she opened the door. He came in and relocked it.

"Did you catch him?" She searched his face.

"No. He managed to slip outside without being detected by the police officers."

Her shoulders slumped. "How does he keep doing that? And how did he get into the house in the first place?"

"We have to consider the possibility that Blake might have hired someone to help with his plan, with or without Renee's knowledge. It's the only thing that makes sense. I'm going to check in with Luke."

Trent retrieved his phone from the bed and dialed. The call didn't go through. A niggle of unease started in his stomach. "The storm must be messing with cell service."

He switched on the radio on top of the dresser. Storms were frequent in the area, and it wasn't unheard of for the power to go out as well as cell service. It was a good idea to keep a radio to pick up local stations.

The weather service had issued a flash flood warning for the entire county because of the already-soaked ground. There was a good chance the river would overflow its banks and flood the roads. They'd be stuck without any means of escape.

Someone knocked on the door.

Trent grabbed his weapon to answer it.

Jacob stepped into the room. "One of the officers came and told us most of them are being pulled away to help with the massive flooding taking place across town. They're having to evacuate homes, and they're short-staffed already with the search for the missing woman." He peered past Trent to where a terrified Eve listened in. "I thought you should both know."

It was the worst possible news. When Jacob started to leave, Trent stopped him. "Hold on a second. Do you and Samuel still own weapons?"

Jacob took his time answering. "We do."

"You think he'll come back," Eve said as if reading his mind.

It wasn't unlikely considering the criminal's behavior so far. "We can't afford to dismiss the possibility."

Jacob shook his head. "This is some mess." He hesitated, then said, "Listen, I didn't want to say this in front of you, Evie, but do you think this could be your father?"

Eve recoiled as if Jacob had struck her.

"I know it's hard to imagine," Jacob continued. "But he's smart and he's been missing for a while. Maybe he staged the whole explosion to cover up suspicion and make us think someone was coming after him. Eve could have seen him and blocked out the memory. Once it comes to light, Henry will be in a lot of trouble. He'd have reason to want your memories to stay buried, Eve."

"We don't know anything for certain," Trent said, in an attempt to make her feel better. "No need to jump to any conclusions."

"You're right. I don't know what I'm saying. Sorry, Evie." Jacob stepped out into the hall once more. "I'm going to get our weapons from the safe and check on Mom and Betsy." Jacob held the lantern high as he descended the steps.

Once he was out of sight, Trent closed the door and locked it. The phone in Trent's hand rang. "It's Luke." He brought it up to his ear. "Boy, am I happy to hear from you. I'm here with Eve. Service has been out for a bit." He put the phone on speaker.

"I know. I've been trying to reach you. I'm sorry we had to call in our officers, but the storm is wreaking havoc. We may have an all-out evacuation in several areas. How are things there?"

"Not good." Trent told Luke about the latest attack.

"Good grief. How did he get inside the house in the first place?"

"That's what we're all wondering," Trent said.

Luke paused for a second before delivering another blow. "I'm afraid I have some more bad news. When my men left the property, they told me the river was overflowing its banks. It won't be long before the property floods. The road is probably gone by now."

In other words, they were on their own. Trent ran his hand across his eyes.

"What about Blake?" Eve asked. "Were you able to tie him to the attacks on me?"

The length of time it took Luke to respond wasn't encouraging. "No, and we grilled him hard. We had him account for every second of his time, going back before you arrived. His alibis check out. He was actually working at the furniture factory during most of that time frame. He told Renee he was taking photos, and he was, but he's also been working at the factory to bring in money because I guess his photos aren't selling. We checked his time cards and the factory's surveillance. I'm afraid we have to rule him out as your attacker, Eve."

They were back to square one. "And Renee?" Trent asked in frustration. "She was pretty mad when she left here, and she's obviously got it in for Eve for some reason. I realize she couldn't do it alone, but maybe she hired someone."

Trent glanced at Eve. All he wanted was to tell her everything was going to be okay, yet they were still no closer to identifying the person trying to harm her.

"We're working on it. She's staying with her friend in town. I have one of my people watching the place. She's not directly responsible for the recent attack, but it's possible she could have hired someone. We'll keep both Renee and Blake under close watch, but there's something else going on here."

Trent agreed. And they'd better figure it out soon. "Any word on the missing woman?"

Luke released a sigh that was answer enough. "No, and as we both know, if this is the Roadside Stalker, she doesn't have much longer."

The killer normally kept his victims alive for less than forty-eight hours. The clock was ticking on the woman's life.

"I almost forgot," Luke said. "Blake mentioned something strange. He claimed someone had used his vehicle before and left the seat in a different position. The car was kept at his place in town with the keys under the floor mat."

"In other words, anyone could have used it." Trent watched desperation pass over Eve's face as he related Jacob's theory about Henry being the perp.

"Even though he left his family, I can't see Henry harming his daughter. Still, it's worth checking into. I'll get started and if I find anything, I'll let you know. But in the meantime—"

"I know, I know." Trent clasped Eve's hand. "Be safe."

"I mean it, Trent. Eve's attacker is still on the loose, and we can't yet rule out the possibility that this is all part of the serial killer case. You can't be too careful."

"Copy that." Trent ended the call. Things were spinning out of control, leading to a showdown that was rooted in the past, and the list of possible perps seemed endless.

"We'll be fine here," he said to Eve, knowing she didn't believe it any more than he did. But she was scared enough. She didn't need to see his uncertainty.

"Will we?" she challenged. "Because I'm not so sure."

As he racked his brain for a comforting response, the alarm on his phone beeped. Something had triggered one of the security monitors.

"What's going on?" she asked as he studied the screen.

Trent could see a figure dressed entirely in black moving around near the camera. "Someone is trespassing on the property." And there were no longer any police officers around to investigate. If that was the perp targeting Eve, then he'd fallen back to wait for his next chance, and he'd probably seen the police leave. "I have to check it out."

He grabbed the extra weapon he'd tucked inside his bag and handed it to Eve. "I need you to go to your room and lock the door. Stand watch at the window. If you see anyone who shouldn't be here, shoot." He met her eye as he said the last part. Eve was proficient with a gun and knew how to disable someone without causing them deadly harm. "I'll have Jacob and Samuel take turns watching this floor as well."

Trent confirmed no one was out in the hall before he escorted her back to her room. "Lock up and stay safe."

Before he could step from the room, Eve stopped him. He gazed into her eyes and saw love mingled with concern. He did his best not to let his emotions go down that path again, when it would almost certainly lead to heartbreak.

He failed, and he knew it.

Trent framed her face with his hands and leaned down to kiss her tenderly.

While he may not have known what the future held, he would always love her, and he would lay down his life without hesitation to protect her.

17

Without a word, he stepped out of the room and closed the door quietly. His absence seeped into her soul. She'd wanted to tell him she loved him. Wanted to say she was sorry for leaving all those years ago without so much as an explanation. But none of the words had come out, and he was gone.

Eve listened to his footsteps fading. She touched her finger to her lips where he'd kissed her. "I love you," she whispered. "Please don't let it be too late."

She clutched the weapon in one hand and the lantern he'd given her in the other. With the power out, her once-inviting childhood room took on an ominous glow. Her body craved sleep. The exhaustion of the past few days weighed on her, but until she knew for certain that Trent was safe, it was impossible to think about her own needs.

Eve set the lantern on her dresser and went over to the window. Nothing stirred below. Was her attacker the one who had set off the alarm? Her thoughts continued to bounce from Trent and their unknown future to the person trying to kill her. What terrible things were still locked away in her memory to make someone want her dead? She pressed her balled fist against her forehead. "Remember." She closed her eyes, and yet the rest of the memories from that night refused to be released.

When she opened her eyes, she noticed that her old teddy bear had remained in its place since the night she'd left this room for the last time.

The bear had been a gift from her father, which made it even more precious. But after the way her father discarded his family, when Eve's grandmother had asked what things she wanted packed up and sent to her new home in Syracuse, "Teddy" hadn't been included.

The room seemed suspended in time. Same bedspread as before. The same photos on the wall reflecting her teenage dreams. Her books and magazine were displayed where she'd left them, as if her grandmother had wanted everything to be the same in case her granddaughter ever came home.

It broke Eve's heart to think of the hurt she'd caused her grandparents, and her uncles and Betsy, by refusing to return.

She studied the soggy world below her window. *Please keep Trent safe*, she prayed.

The desire to call her mother and hear her voice was great. Eve looked around the room, but her phone was gone. When the power had gone out, she'd run from the room and almost died. Trent had come to her rescue and taken her to his room, but she hadn't brought her phone with her. So where was it?

A sliver of fear worked its way through her frame. To her knowledge, her attacker hadn't entered the room. Eve searched the bed and then beneath it in case she'd dropped the phone somehow, but it wasn't there. She had no way to call the outside world or get in touch with Trent should something happen.

She struggled to remain calm. Everything would be fine. Her uncles were in the house. They'd be up soon to guard her. Eve went back to the bed and sat on the edge. She picked up Teddy and held him against her chest. Tears filled her eyes as she thought about how much she'd loved the stuffed bear, simply because it was a gift from her father.

On the nightstand sat a photo of her mother and father and Eve skiing the year before the explosion. She picked it up. They'd been so happy. Eve beamed up at her father as her mother watched with amusement and love. If only she'd known back then the terrible things that awaited her family, things that would tear them apart forever.

She set the photo facedown. With the power out, long shadows flickered around the edges of the light like ghosts playing a macabre game.

A noise outside her room grabbed her attention. It sounded like something being dragged down the hall. Eve's heart kicked out a frenzied beat as she ran to the door and put her ear against it.

"Samuel? Jacob?"

No answer. The noise had stopped. Had she imagined it? She was on edge and jumping at every little sound.

Eve waited near the door. Silence.

She returned to the bed and closed her eyes, willing herself to remember.

Recollection flashed through her mind. Someone had fled the back of the garage when she'd gone around to investigate. He'd caught sight of her and stopped, almost as if he had been hesitating, then he'd waved his hands wildly. "Run!" he'd called to her. She'd heard his voice.

Her eyes shot open, and the memory vanished.

Eve tried again to bring the image back but it was gone. She could think of one reason someone would warn her. She wasn't the target—her father was. They were coming after her because she could identify them. Perspiration beaded on her forehead. Her heart rate picked up as she swallowed several times, but her mouth felt as dry as the desert.

As long as she'd stayed away, she posed no threat. But now that she was back, the killer believed it was simply a matter of time before she identified them.

Beyond the door, the sound of something being dragged started up again, but louder and closer. She bit back a scream.

Her heart leaped to her throat. "Jacob? Is that you?" She paused, listening, but heard only silence. "Samuel?"

Her eyes were glued to the door. If the stalker was trying to get into her room, she was trapped without a phone, and the lone way out was the window on the second floor of the house.

A heavy object slammed against her door.

She jumped to her feet and glanced at the bottom of the door. Light danced beneath it as if someone were shuffling around. And then something far more disturbing than the person outside her room wafted under the door.

Smoke! But why weren't the alarms going off—unless someone had disabled them?

"Help!" she screamed at the top of her lungs. "Help me, please!" There was no answer. Where were her uncles and Betsy? Her grandmother? "Is anyone there?"

She struggled not to give in to panic. Keeping a clear head would be critical to staying alive.

Smoke snaked into the room, assaulting her eyes and nose. Through tears streaming down her face, Eve shoved as hard as she could, but the door wouldn't budge.

She was trapped inside. The one way out was the window.

Her stomach clenched when she thought about what that would entail. But she wanted to live. She couldn't let this be the end.

Eve ran to the window. There was nothing below it. She would have to hang from the windowsill and drop down, in an attempt to reduce the amount of distance she fell.

She struggled to lift the window, but it refused to budge.

"No, no, no." She tried again with the same result. She peered through the window and found that someone had nailed it shut from outside, trapping her inside.

A sob escaped. *Don't fall apart*, she ordered herself. *Think!*

She scrubbed at her damp cheeks. There had to be something she could do. The room was filling with smoke. If she could break the window, she could get some fresh air. It was too high up to jump from, but maybe she could scream loud enough to get someone's attention.

Eve aimed the weapon and prepared to shoot out the window, but another noise sounded outside her room. Scuffling sounds.

Someone screamed, followed by a loud thud.

She focused on the door, weapon ready. If her attacker was about to break in, he would find out that she wouldn't go down without a fight. She'd fought so hard to remember that night, to fit the pieces together, but she hadn't been able to, and now it was too late.

Outside the room, the object blocking the door crashed to the floor. Eve screamed and backed away. She'd forgotten to relock the door when Trent left.

Eve gripped the gun tight as the door swung open.

A figure stepped into the room, a cloth covering the bottom half of his face. The part of the room near the door was clouded by smoke, and with his face partially covered, she couldn't make out anything about him other than that he was tall. And familiar.

"Stay back." The words were choked in a fit of coughing. It was becoming a struggle to breathe. Through the tears streaming from her eyes, she pointed the gun at the figure advancing on her.

And then she saw enough of his face to know. The gun fell from her hand as she clutched the teddy bear tighter in the other.

It had been twelve years and he had aged a good deal. There were streaks of gray throughout his hair and lines around his eyes. But she would have known him anywhere.

"Dad?"

He removed the cloth from his face and coughed several times before he could speak. "Yes, it's me. We have to hurry, Eve. The house is engulfed. Samuel set the fire to stop me from getting to you." He reached for her arm.

She couldn't believe what he said. She yanked out of his grasp.

The smoke continued to assault her nose and throat. Eve coughed violently as the thick air surrounded her. "Why would Uncle Samuel try to kill me? What are you doing here?" Nothing about any of it made sense.

"I'll explain everything once you're safe. Hurry, Eve. I have to get the others out too. Please." He went to the bathroom and returned, holding out a soaked hand towel for her.

She stared at him, and her heart decided almost without her involvement. He was her father. He was the man she'd always known him to be. She nodded. "Okay."

"Stay behind me," Henry said. They stepped from her room into smoke so thick it was hard to see anything.

Her father stopped suddenly and she slammed into him.

"He's gone," he choked out, spinning toward her. "Samuel and I fought. I had to knock him out to get to you. But he's gone now."

The man who had tried to kill her could be waiting anywhere within the smoke-filled house, to finish the job. Eve realized she'd left the gun in her room, but it would be sealing her death to try and go back for it.

"Come, Eve. We have to get out of the house now. It's too dangerous."

The landing appeared in front of them. The thought of trying to descend the stairs when she couldn't see much was terrifying, and her father sensed it.

"Take my hand," he told her, as he had so many times in the past. Growing up, whenever she was scared and too afraid to do something alone, he would tell her to take his hand. She'd always felt safe as long as her hand was tucked in his. Her father wouldn't let anything happen to her.

Eve slipped her hand into his.

"I've got you, sweetheart. Follow me."

With her heart in her throat, she followed him. They stepped from the landing onto the first step and Eve lost her footing and stumbled against him.

Henry stopped to steady her. "Are you okay?"

"Yes, I'm okay." Her voice shook. "Let's keep going. The sooner we're out, the better."

Step by excruciatingly slow step, they descended the stairs.

When they reached the final one, Eve blew out a relieved breath. It felt as if they'd descended Mount Everest.

Her father pulled her around to his side and started toward the front door.

As he opened it, rain-drenched fresh air reached them on a gust of wind. Eve dropped the towel as she and her father stumbled from the house. She doubled over, coughing the smoke from her lungs.

"I'm going back for the others," her father said, handing her his phone. "Call for help."

"Dad, no!"

But before she could stop him, he disappeared inside the smoke-filled house.

With shaking fingers, Eve dialed 911 and told the dispatcher everything as quickly as she could.

"We have officers on the way now," the dispatcher said, "but the road is out so we have to send in the chopper. Are you safe at the moment?"

Eve glanced around the darkness. "I don't know where my uncle is."

"Is there someplace you can go to get out of sight?" the dispatcher asked.

She spotted Jacob. He had to know what his brother had done. Jacob could be in jeopardy as well.

"I'm safe for now," she assured the dispatcher. "There's no sign of the person who set the fire. Please hurry."

"Help is on the way. Stay on the phone with me until they arrive."

With the phone in her hand, Eve ran to Jacob and hugged him close.

Her uncle returned the embrace. "Thank goodness you're safe."

"My father is inside," Eve told him. "He went back for the rest of the family. Samuel set the fire." She stared at the house, terrified that just when she'd gotten him back, her father would succumb to the smoke that filled the air.

"Samuel. I-I can't believe it." Jacob appeared astonished. "Why would my brother do such a thing?"

Eve coughed some more. Her voice was hoarse from inhaling smoke. "I don't know, but we have to help my father. He could be trapped there. He's been inside for a while."

"The rest of the family are in the barn. It's far enough away from the house that it should be safe. I'll take you to them and then I'll go back for him."

He kept his arm around her shoulders.

Eve hesitated. She didn't want to leave her father. She'd lost him once, and she didn't want to lose him again.

"Eve, hurry. I have to go back for your father."

She nodded hesitantly.

He started around the side of the house—away from the barn.

"Where are we going?" she asked and tried to stop, but he pulled her on. "I thought you said they were in the barn."

A strange smile spread across his face. "They are, but I think I saw your father near the side door."

Startled, Eve jerked toward it. "Where?"

"I saw him," Jacob insisted. "He's over there. And he's hurt. Come, Eve. We must help him."

The arm around her tightened, and he started for the door at a fast pace without letting her hesitate.

Eve's distressed gaze searched the shadows around the house. She didn't see her father. Had Jacob been wrong? Had he been *lying*?

Windows in the house exploded, sending glass shattering around them. But the door was shut.

"Jacob, he's not here. We have to help him." She pulled away and started toward the front of the house.

"Eve! Eve, where are you?" her father shouted from the front of the house.

Her father had never been around the side of the house. If he went back inside to search for her and the others, he might die.

"He's looking for me," Eve insisted, as Jacob grabbed her again. "I don't want him to think I've gone back inside." She struggled to free herself. "What are you doing?" The rest of her words died away when she saw Jacob's malevolent expression.

He was not the man who had been her friend for years, who had listened to her fears and her hopes for the future.

Jacob raised his hand and slapped her hard. "You foolish girl. You have no idea the trouble you've caused me."

She clutched her stinging cheek as her eyes widened in horror and realization.

In the fire's glow, she spotted the spider tattoo on his hand, and the final memory from the night of the explosion clicked into place. She'd seen it so many times since then, giving little thought to the symbol on her uncle's skin, but it hadn't registered before. Between the fire, the tattoo, and the rage on his face, the pieces came together.

Jacob had called out to her to run away twelve years ago—he'd been the one fleeing from the garage that night. Jacob had set the explosion that killed Christy because he was trying to kill her father before Henry could expose him to the police.

Jacob was the one who had been trying to kill Eve all along.

The betrayal was crushing. No wonder her mind had blocked it out for over a decade.

"No, oh no. Why, Jacob?"

"Why do you think?" he snarled. "If your father had kept his nose out of it, none of this would have happened. It's all his fault."

The chains on her memory had shattered and bits of the argument she'd overheard in her grandfather's office broke free of their restraints.

It had been Samuel she'd overheard arguing with her father. Henry had told Samuel he was going to the police with evidence that Jacob had been stealing from the family business. Samuel had urged him to wait until he'd spoken to Jacob. It was then that the call had come in and her father stormed out of the office, never realizing what dangerous plot was being formed against him.

Eve once again tried to free herself, but Jacob's hold tightened. His free hand snaked around her throat. "If it weren't for Henry's meddling, I would have gotten away with everything."

She grabbed his fingers around her throat and tried to pry them away.

"Lucky for me, he trusted Samuel and told him what he'd found." A maniacal grin creased Jacob's face. "Henry had no idea Samuel was in on it with me." Jacob laughed cruelly and pressed down harder on her throat, cutting off her air.

In a panic, she clawed at his face and kicked him with her dwindling strength, but no matter how hard she fought, she was no match for a madman set on covering up his crimes.

18

Trent reached the spot where the camera had sensed motion, but it was too late. Someone had dismantled all the security cameras, and there was a single set of footprints around the spot.

The truth became clear—Trent had been lured out of the house.

He'd left Eve, and she was in danger. He spun toward the house and spotted smoke billowing up through the trees.

His heart leaped to his throat.

Trent raced through the woods as fast as his legs would carry him, with soaked tree branches slapping at his face. Arms pumping at his sides, he ignored everything but the task of getting to Eve. He reached the house in record time and was shocked to find Henry standing out front. Trent remembered what Jacob had said about Henry being responsible for the money stolen from the Lourdeses' company, and he grabbed the older man's shoulders.

"Where is she? Tell me what you've done to her."

Henry's features twisted in confusion. "She's not inside. I got her out. I tried to go back and search for the others but the fire and smoke were too much. She and the rest of the family must have moved into the woods."

"I just came from the woods. There's no one there." Desperation threatened to take control. He had to find her.

Trent raced around the side of the house when movement caught his attention. To his horror, he caught sight of Eve's back, and someone's hands wrapped around her neck as she struggled to break free.

"Stop!" he yelled, rushing toward them. The strangler jerked around at the sound of Trent's voice. The sheer horror at seeing Jacob attacking Eve almost buckled Trent's legs as he ran. The man was not the Jacob he knew. Trent bolted forward and grabbed hold of him.

"Get off me!" Jacob roared, fighting to free himself from Trent's hold. The rage on his face was hard to associate with the kind image he'd always presented to those around him.

"Let her go." With a mighty effort, Trent pulled him off of Eve, who fell to the ground.

"Stay out of my way," Jacob snarled.

Trent shoved him back.

Jacob lunged toward Eve with a snarl.

Trent drew his weapon. "That's close enough."

Jacob froze, eyeing the weapon.

"I don't want to shoot you, but I will," Trent said coldly.

Keeping an eye on Eve's uncle, Trent eased over to Eve. "Did he hurt you?" He'd almost lost her.

She coughed violently, then buried her face in his shoulder. "I don't think so. I can't believe Jacob tried to kill me," she said with a sob.

Trent held her closer. "He had us all fooled."

Henry rounded the corner and spotted Trent holding the gun on Jacob. He didn't seem surprised. Henry stepped in front of Jacob, his eyes flashing with anger. "You tried to kill me—and my daughter."

Jacob's contempt-filled gaze swept over Henry. "I did what I had to do to protect myself and my brother. You were always trouble. My dad hated you. So did Samuel and I. You deserved everything you got, and you should have stayed gone."

Henry jerked back at the malice on Jacob's face. "I left because you threatened Eve's life and her mother's. You promised if I stayed away, you would leave them alone. But you didn't." Henry's hands fisted at his sides. Trent had no doubt he was struggling to keep from striking Jacob.

What Henry said finally sank in. "Did you say he threatened Eve and Melanie?" Trent asked.

Before Henry had the chance to answer, a police helicopter, with its spotlights trained on the blazing house, searched for a place to land.

"That's Luke." Trent had never been happier to see his friend. He caught hold of Jacob as a precaution, handing his gun to Eve to keep trained on her uncle.

Once the chopper landed, Luke and several officers exited. They spotted Trent holding Jacob captive and approached with handcuffs.

Jacob spotted the cuffs and fought to free himself while alternately blaming Henry and Eve for his crimes. He broke free, but was quickly taken down and cuffed. The officers led him away while he continued to struggle against the restraints.

"This is all your fault, Eve," he raged. "If you had just stayed away, I wouldn't have had to try to kill you."

Trent wondered if, in his twisted mind, Jacob actually bought his own lies.

"Samuel is involved in this as well," Trent told Luke. "We have to find him."

Jane and Betsy had emerged from the family barn and ran toward them. Both women hugged Eve tight.

"I was so worried," Jane told her granddaughter. "We got out when we smelled smoke. We thought you'd be right behind us." Her eyes widened when she spotted Henry. "What are you doing here? Where are Samuel and Jacob?" She searched the smoky darkness for her sons.

"We don't know where Samuel is, but Jacob is in the helicopter." Eve pulled away and put her arm around Jane's shoulders as she relayed the truth.

Jane's expression changed from concern to horror in an instant. "No, it's not possible. They wouldn't do such a thing." Jane stared at her granddaughter as if hoping she would say it was all a mistake.

"I'm sorry, Gran, but it is."

Jane collapsed against her and wept.

Sirens could be heard in the distance, heading their direction. "The fire department is on the way. We had to find a different route to get them over the water," Luke said, studying the raging flames. "I'm afraid there will be no saving the house." He pulled out a notepad and pen. "Well, Mr. Cameron, I understand you have a lot to tell me."

As Henry explained his side, it soon became clear that Jacob had been taking money from the Lourdeses' logging business for years and funneling it to different banks in the Cayman Islands.

"I thought it was Jacob alone at first, but it's becoming clearer that Samuel was in on it too. They both realized I was tracking down the missing funds and tried to frame me for it." Henry shook his head. "And it worked. Alfred fired me. No matter how much I tried to explain, that stubborn old man wouldn't listen." He looked at Eve. "I'm so, so sorry, honey. I really messed things up. Samuel made me think he was going to talk to his brother and get him to turn himself in to Alfred and straighten things out. Instead, he told Jacob and then—"

"Then the explosion happened," Eve finished for him. She held her grandmother close. "It was meant for you, Dad."

Henry had been an innocent victim of that night's events, just like Christy and Eve.

Two police officers approached with a soaked and sullen Samuel between them.

"We found him hiding in the woods," one officer told them.

"Take him to the chopper with his brother," Luke instructed.

The fire department arrived on the scene, though it was only a matter of containing the flames by then.

"Let's get everyone out of the rain." Trent took Eve's hand, and together they moved to the barn, with Jane and Betsy close by.

He noticed something on the ground and bent over to pick it up. It was Eve's old teddy bear. He handed it to her.

"Oh, good. You found where I hid the thumb drive." Henry pointed to the bear.

"What are you talking about?" Eve asked, her brows knit together in a frown. She glanced down at the bear in her arms. "I must have brought this out with me. I didn't realize I was still holding it."

"Good thing too," Henry said. "I hid the thumb drive containing the information I'd shown Samuel, along with more detailed records of the missing funds, in Teddy. I was concerned Jacob and Samuel would find it if they searched Alfred's office. When they threatened me, I had to leave before I could retrieve it, but there should be enough information on the drive to convict them."

Eve handed the bear to Luke. "I guess you'll need this."

"Thank you. We'll get this back to you soon. Henry, if you don't mind, I'd like for you to come with us to the station to get your story down."

"No problem." Henry stepped closer to his daughter. "I never stopped loving you, Eve, or your mother. I'm so sorry I've put you through all this. I never meant to put you in harm's way." He cupped her face with one hand. "I've missed you so much."

Trent watched with an aching heart as Eve listened to her father, her eyes filling with tears.

Henry continued. "But Jacob threatened to harm you both if I stayed or went to the police, and I'd seen what he was capable of. When Melanie announced she was moving you to Syracuse, I was happy because I thought you'd be safe." He shook his head. "Through the years, I watched over you both from afar. I was there in disguise when you graduated from university, but I didn't dare show myself. It broke my heart not to be able to be with you and Melanie each day, but I thought I was doing what was best for you both."

Shocked gasps emitted from Jane and Betsy. Jane appeared to be frozen from the trauma of hearing that her sons were responsible for so many crimes, while Betsy quietly wept over her husband's actions.

Henry's eyes pleaded with Eve to understand, but she appeared to struggle as she tried to absorb all the new information.

"I'm sorry, Jane. Betsy. I know this is hard to hear." Henry nodded at the two women. "I never wanted to divide your family." Facing Eve once more, he continued, "When I realized you were returning to Lourdes Mansion, I was terrified of what Jacob would do to you. He'd already tried to kill me and he'd threatened your life." He shook his head.

"Who was the call from, the night of the explosion?" Trent asked.

"I thought it was from our accountant, but now I realize it was Jacob disguising his voice. He told me he needed to speak to me right away at the office. It should have been me who died that night," he said, visibly shaken. "Instead, he killed Christy and hurt you, Eve."

Eve reached for her father's hand. "You had no way of knowing what Jacob would do."

Henry clasped hers tight. "I almost lost you once. I couldn't let that happen again."

With the information Henry had on the thumb drive, Trent was positive they could finally solve the mystery of the explosion, and put Samuel and Jacob away.

"That night, I spotted Jacob around back and went to investigate," Eve said in a rough whisper. "He told me to run, and I saw the tattoo on his hand. It stood out in my mind because Jacob had only recently gotten it, and he was so proud of it. He showed it off all the time."

She shook her head. "Then he hit me with something and—" Her voice trailed off.

Trent's gaze narrowed. They'd all thought Eve had been thrown by the explosion and struck her head, but it had all been Jacob.

"The blast threw both of us. I was knocked unconscious." She shrugged. "Jacob must have run away."

"And I'm guessing Jacob is the one who used Blake's car, hoping to throw suspicion onto Blake and Renee." Luke added, glancing over to where the fire department worked to contain the blaze. "Let's get you all out of here. We'll take your statements once we're down at the station."

"I have a house in town," Trent reminded them. "Everyone is welcome to stay with me for as long as you need to."

Trent kept a close eye on Eve as she helped her grandmother and Betsy into the chopper, where Samuel and Jacob were being restrained by cuffs, an officer on each side.

Betsy avoided eye contact with her husband. Trent couldn't imagine her surprise at learning that the man she loved had helped commit murder.

Trent sat beside Eve, who also appeared to be in a state of shock.

"We should have your throat examined once we reach town," he murmured.

She nodded. "It's so hard to wrap my mind around any of this." Her hoarse voice was little more than a whisper.

"Don't try to talk," he told her. "I know it's hard, but we'll figure it all out. We have the people responsible in custody."

A single tear slipped from her eye, and he put an arm around her to let her cry on his shoulder.

"Have you finally remembered everything?" he asked gently.

She nodded. "It's awful."

He held her tighter and was content to simply be in the moment with her. There were things coming down the pike that were going to be hard for her to cope with, but he'd be there for her through all of it.

Several minutes later, the chopper circled the helipad near the station. Once it landed, Samuel and Jacob were led away.

"I want to go with my sons," Jane told Luke firmly. "No matter what they've done, they are still my children."

"Yes ma'am." Luke escorted her to the station.

Betsy held back. "I'm so ashamed. I had no idea my husband was capable of such terrible things. How can I ever be around the family again?"

Eve embraced her aunt. "You are family too, and you aren't responsible for what Samuel and Jacob did."

"But I should have known." She wiped her eyes. "I should have sensed that my husband was up to something."

Trent's heart went out to her. "Samuel had everyone convinced he was a caring person. We never could have imagined what he and Jacob were doing. They fooled us all."

Betsy sniffled. "Why would they do such a thing? Alfred was a generous man. They never wanted for anything."

It was something Trent couldn't understand either. Alfred's sons had always been a bit spoiled, but Trent wouldn't have thought them capable of going to such extreme lengths for more money than they already had. And he regretted suspecting that Renee had been responsible.

"I still love him," Betsy said, her chin trembling. "Despite everything, I still love him. I should get him a lawyer."

"I know you love him," Eve said in a tight voice. "But after what he and Jacob have done, it will be a long time before I can find it in my heart to forgive them."

Betsy nodded. "In the meantime, are you and I all right?"

Eve smiled and took her aunt's hand. "Of course."

When they entered the station, Luke spotted them and came over. "Jacob and Samuel are being processed," he told Betsy. "Jane has asked to speak to them after they've been questioned. If you want to talk with your husband, you can."

"Thank you," Betsy murmured.

"Why don't I get you some coffee?" Trent offered. "It could be a while before you're able to speak with Samuel."

"That would be nice." Betsy spotted Jane and went over to her mother-in-law. Trent had no doubt she and Jane would have a heart-to-heart like the one Betsy had just had with Eve.

"Those two men have destroyed their family," Luke growled. He faced Eve. "I have the EMTs coming to take a look at you."

She smiled gratefully. "Thank you."

Luke pressed her arm. "I'd better go. As soon as I have more news, I'll let you all know."

When Eve and Trent were alone, a strained silence came between them.

"Let's get Jane and Betsy some coffee," Trent suggested.

She glanced at her family and agreed. "They tried to kill me, my father, you—all for money."

There were still so many unanswered questions in Trent's mind as well. Why had Jacob and Samuel chosen to imitate the Stalker, and where was the missing girl?

In the break room, he started a fresh pot of coffee and rolled his shoulders to release the pressure that had been building there since he'd come across Eve on the road.

Once the coffee finished brewing, Trent poured two cups. He was about to ask if she wanted one, when he caught sight of her quaking shoulders and set the cups down.

"Hey, it's going to be okay." He wrapped his arms around her. How he loved her. Had always loved her. He hoped she realized how much, how he'd give anything to protect her for the rest of their days.

"No, it isn't. I've spent my adult life blaming and resenting my dad for leaving us," she said with a sob.

"How could you know the truth?"

"I should have trusted him. I knew who he really was, and I should have assumed he had a good reason," Eve said. "He sacrificed everything because he was afraid for our safety if he stayed or tried to turn them in."

Trent rested his chin on her head. "But you have a second chance—you all do. It's possible to rebuild your relationship."

She sniffed, then pulled away. "That's true. You know, for so long, every time I thought about Lourdes Mansion, all I could think about was that night, losing Christy and my dad in one fell swoop." She shook her head. "I was so hurt and angry. I wanted to forget everything, sever all my connections here. That's why I ended things with you. I knew I couldn't live here anymore, and I couldn't ask you to leave."

The words were like a punch to the gut. Their lives would have been so different if she'd trusted him with the truth back then.

She captured a strand of hair and tucked it behind her ear. "Now that I know the truth, it's as if all of that ugliness has been set free, as if it's no longer here." She waved her hand. "But it's too late. Everything is gone."

Hope took root in his heart, but still he hesitated. Did he dare tell her the truth—that it was anything but over for him?

He gazed into her eyes and saw the future he'd always wanted. He hadn't fought to stand with her when she left. He would never let her leave again, not if he could convince her to stay.

"It doesn't have to be," he told her.

She tilted her head with a curious expression. "But it is gone. The house. The family."

He shook his head, trying to hide his disappointment. "It isn't. It's in your heart. This isn't the first time the house has been damaged. And it's just that—a house. Home is what you make it. It's where your heart is."

She turned away. "I don't know if I'm that strong."

Trent barely caught the words. She had doubts, but he didn't.

"You are, Eve. I promise you are." He picked up the cups. "Come on. Let's take these to your grandmother and aunt. I think they both need our strength now."

He walked beside her without speaking, but his thoughts were crashing together. He'd found her again after a twelve-year period in which he'd been sleepwalking through life. Beyond promising Samantha's family that he would find her killer, part of the reason he'd become so obsessed with the case was that Samantha had always reminded him of Eve.

He loved Eve. And now that she was here again, he couldn't let her walk away from him without trying to make things work.

Trent vowed to fight for her this time—no matter what.

19

Luke stepped out of an interrogation room, accompanied by Eve's father. Eve, Trent, Gran, and Betsy rose to meet them as they approached.

"What's happening with my sons?" Gran asked, her eyes latching onto Luke's.

Eve wrapped her arm around her grandmother's waist. She'd suffered so much already, and Eve wished she could take the burden from her.

"Samuel and Jacob are speaking with their attorneys, but they've agreed to give statements. As soon as we have those, I'll allow you both to speak with them," Luke assured her.

"Thank you, Luke." The somber tone of Gran's voice worried Eve. Her grandmother's shoulders stooped as if the weight of the world rested on her alone.

Eve led her back to her chair. "Why don't you and Betsy rest while we wait?" She returned to Luke and Trent, who were speaking quietly with her father. "I want to listen in when they give their statements," Eve told Luke.

"I don't think that's a good idea, sweetheart," her father said. He was trying to shield her from the ugly details that would be revealed.

She loved him for it, but she had to hear what they'd done from their mouths. "I have to, Dad." Calling him that came as easily as it had in her childhood.

He finally relented. "I want to be there with you." He looked at Trent. "And I'd like for you to be there as well."

"Of course," Trent agreed.

"I'll come to get you when we're ready," Luke told them before leaving.

Trent pressed Eve's shoulder before stepping away, as if he sensed there were things father and daughter needed to talk about alone.

"I should call Mom. She must be going out of her mind with worry." Eve had left her phone behind when the power went out, lost now, surely, to the house fire.

"Use mine." Her father handed it to her, then hesitated. "And please—tell your mother how sorry I am."

Eve studied her father's wounded face before wrapping her arms around him and holding him close.

"No, Dad, you have nothing to be sorry for. You're a victim too." Her voice broke, and the emotions she'd held onto for so long came rushing out.

Her father's arms tightened around her. "I should have found a way to bring them down sooner. I should have protected you better."

She couldn't let him blame himself. "You did what you thought you had to do, to protect me and Mom."

"I love you, Evie," he said in a voice thick with emotion. "I can't tell you how much I've missed you and your mother. How much I've longed for us to be a family again, but I have no right to ask that much, of you or of Melanie."

She pulled away to gaze into his face. "I want that too. I can't speak for Mom, but I have my father back, and I don't plan to lose you again."

"I'm so glad." He nodded toward Trent. "What about him?"

Eve knew what he was asking, but she'd made too many mistakes with Trent. "He deserves better," she said. "I broke things off without giving an explanation. Trent didn't deserve that."

Henry held her close. "You're right. He didn't. But that's the beauty of second chances. If you get one, you do everything in your power to not make the same mistakes again. I can see you still love him. Make it right, Evie. I know you can."

Eve so wanted to let herself hope that she could have that second chance with Trent, but certainly her father was simply trying to comfort her to make up for the years he'd missed.

She stepped away to call her mother. "Mom, it's me," she said as soon as Melanie answered.

"Eve! Oh, honey, I've been so worried! I've been trying to call you for hours. Are you okay?"

Eve pulled in a breath and did her best to explain what had transpired. "Mom, Dad's here. You see, he didn't want to leave. He did it to keep us safe from Samuel and Jacob."

"I-I can't believe it," her mother breathed out, in a voice Eve almost didn't recognize. "Why didn't he tell us? Me? We could have helped him."

Eve looked at her father, standing close by. "Why don't I let him tell you?" She held out the phone for him to take.

Her father hesitated. "I don't know how to fix it," he whispered. "What if she doesn't want to hear what I have to say?"

Eve smiled gently. "You'll never know if you don't try."

He accepted the phone. "Hello, Melanie."

Eve went back to the others.

"How is he?" Trent asked. He'd been watching their exchange. Watching out for her like he always did.

"He'll be okay. He's speaking to my mom."

She could feel Trent's attention on her face while she pretended to study her father. How could she tell the love of her life that she'd made a terrible mistake letting him go?

"Do you think there's a chance for them to repair their relationship?" he asked.

She forced herself to meet Trent's warm brown eyes. "I sure hope so."

"Eve..."

But before he had the chance to go on, Luke came over. "We're ready to take their statements. We'll interview them separately. Come with me."

Her father ended the call and followed Eve, Trent, and Luke to a smaller room that had a two-way mirror in it.

Luke clicked on the audio to the adjoining room. "You can hear everything from here."

"Thanks, Luke," Eve told him.

With a nod, he left the room.

Soon, Jacob was brought into the interrogation room, along with several police detectives and Luke. An officer attached her uncle's handcuffs to a metal connection on the table.

Luke and two other detectives sat across from Jacob, who faced the two-way mirror.

Jacob's interview, as well as Samuel's, would be recorded. After Luke had gotten on record the identity of everyone in the room, he started the interview. "You've agreed to answer our questions of your own accord, against your attorney's recommendations, correct?"

"Yes, I have," Jacob replied.

"I want to start with what happened twelve years ago, and the missing money," Luke began.

Jacob appeared almost sullen. "It began a long time before that summer. But it was all because of our father." A bitter expression replaced the repentant one.

"What do you mean?"

Eve couldn't take her eyes off Jacob as he told how Grandpa Alfred had grown tired of his and Samuel's extravagant spending. He'd put them both on allowances and tried to teach them the value of working hard, except Jacob hadn't wanted to learn that lesson. Instead, he'd borrowed money from unsavory people at exuberant interest rates to keep up the lifestyle he'd become accustomed to. When the loans came due, Jacob couldn't pay them. He went to Samuel, and together they concocted a plan to take money from the business and create two sets of books to cover their tracks.

"It was only supposed to be temporary until I paid off the loans and we had a little extra in our pockets," Jacob explained.

"What went wrong?" Luke asked.

"A foolish mistake on my part. We used Henry's name on one of the accounts in the Caymans because we thought if anyone ever found out, they'd blame him. And the bank never checked records."

Eve glanced over to her father. He flinched at the careless way Jacob and Samuel had used him.

"But Henry did find out," Luke clarified.

"Yes," Jacob said. "He started nosing around. You see, I was in a rush to complete a late transfer, and I accidentally copied Henry on it."

Such a small, foolish mistake had put her father on a collision course with murder, and had ended Christy's life. All fueled by greed.

"I told Samuel. We had to act fast, so we deleted all the records and then changed the amount of missing money to a much smaller amount. We even transferred the funds to Henry's account and then let Dad know about it. Dad didn't like Henry anyway, so he had no trouble buying that Henry would do such a thing. After he fired Henry, we thought that was the end of it. But Henry wouldn't let it go."

Luke leaned forward. "Let's move forward to the night of the explosion. Tell me about that."

"Henry refused to accept defeat and move on with his life," Jacob ground out in an angry tone. "I offered to help him find a job someplace else. I mean, I didn't like framing him in the first place, but then he wouldn't stop. He'd really dug into the financials. We thought we'd erased all the records, but he found them anyway. Henry had figured out it was me who took the money." Jacob made a derisive sound. "That night, he told Samuel he was going to the police unless I came clean to Dad. He said he had proof it was me." His mouth twisted in a smug grin. "Samuel called me and I faked the call to Henry from the accountant. I looked everywhere for the documents. I searched Henry and Melanie's room but there was nothing. I had no idea they were hidden in Dad's office."

Where it had remained until Grandpa Alfred had found it.

"After the explosion, you told Henry you were the one responsible and you threatened him," Luke prompted.

Jacob's mouth stretched into a cold grin. "That was the easy part. By then, he knew what I was capable of, and I told him if he didn't disappear, the same thing would happen to his precious Evie."

Bile rose in Eve's throat at the careless way her uncle described ruining so many lives to protect himself.

"And all these years, you thought your secrets were safe," Luke said. "But you hadn't counted on Henry inadvertently enlisting help through your dad."

Jacob's smile faltered.

"After your father died, you didn't expect your mother to decide to sell the estate," Luke went on. "When you found out Eve was returning to facilitate the sale, you knew you had to do something. So you tried to run her off the road the night she arrived and make it appear to be a new crime by the Roadside Stalker. When that didn't work, you tried to shoot her, and you didn't care who else you took out in the process."

Jacob's head shot up. "Whoa, hang on a minute. We never tried to run Eve off the road. I don't know what you're talking about. Hang on—does this have something to do with that serial killer from a few years back?"

Luke didn't answer.

Jacob waited for a second longer before continuing. "My brother and I took turns. Samuel was the one who shot at Eve on the night she arrived, and then when she and Trent were on horseback. I pushed her into the river, and followed her and Trent to the office because I thought he might have found the information Henry had on us. We also took a few pieces of art from my father's home office, in an effort to throw off the police."

It was as if the floor beneath her had been removed and Eve was falling.

Was Jacob telling the truth, and the initial attack hadn't been part of his and Samuel's plot to kill her?

"What about in the woods near the caretaker's cabin that second day?" Luke asked.

Jacob shook his head. "That wasn't us."

At her side, Trent stiffened.

"Give me a minute." Luke rose and left the interrogation room. The door opened, and he came into the room where they all stood in shocked disbelief.

"Do you believe him?" Eve asked him.

"I do. He admitted to the other attacks. They didn't run you off the road or attack you in the woods."

Which meant the Stalker had actually targeted her after all.

"I don't understand," Henry said, putting an arm around Eve's shoulders.

Trent crowded close on her other side.

Luke explained about the serial killer who had worked in the area several years before, and about the current missing woman. "I think we have to consider the possibility that Jacob is telling the truth. Eve may have been the Roadside Stalker's original target, but Trent saved her and then Samuel shot at her. The Stalker probably came back the following morning. His plans were foiled again, and so he took another victim."

"So this Stalker has returned to Winter Lake?" Henry asked.

"I'm afraid so," Luke replied grimly. "The task force has been working overtime, but so far, a woman is still missing and—" He stopped. Eve understood that the woman's life was in danger, and it could just as easily have been Eve herself. If her uncles hadn't wanted her dead and created such chaos, the killer might have continued to pursue her.

She shuddered at the thought.

"We'll catch him," Trent assured her. "This time, he's not getting away."

She hoped he was right. Not only for herself, but for that innocent woman out there, enduring who knew what terrible things.

"We have enough to book Jacob. I'm sure Samuel will confirm everything his brother has said. He's already admitted to dismantling the smoke detectors and setting the fire. They'll be charged with murder, attempted murder, theft, and embezzlement, among other things," Luke assured them. "CSI arrived at the estate. They located weapons in the trunk of Samuel's old Mustang that match the shell casings we recovered. And one of the family's four-wheelers was covered in mud like what was found at the place where the shooter was stationed. We should be able to match its tire tracks to those left behind at the scene."

Eve's heart broke for her grandmother and Betsy. Like Christy and Eve's father—and herself—they were innocent victims. So many lives had been forever changed because of Samuel's and Jacob's insatiable greed.

"Oh, and we found something else inside your teddy bear, Eve, besides the copies of the documents you put in there, Henry," Luke told them.

"Like what?" Eve couldn't imagine.

"Like your grandfather's will. It was tucked inside the bear's coat sleeve." Luke glanced around at the curious faces. "Your grandfather made some big changes. He left both the logging and real estate businesses to you, Eve. I think he figured out the truth before he died, and he was determined to keep his sons from destroying everything he'd worked so hard to build."

20

"Why don't we go outside and get some air?" Trent suggested, wanting to give Eve room to breathe and process everything she had learned.

She gave him a lost expression that broke his heart before nodding.

Trent stayed close to her side as they stepped from the station. After all, there was still a killer on the loose. The rain had stopped. A new day had broken, yet a chill clung to the air.

Eve shivered and wrapped her arms around her body in a protective gesture.

"Here." Trent slipped out of his jacket and draped it over her shoulders.

"Thank you." She stared across the street to his office. "I'm having a hard time accepting the fact that my own uncles wanted me dead."

Trent gently turned her to face him. "None of this is your fault, Eve."

A bitter smile lifted the corners of her mouth. "That doesn't make it any easier." Her gaze shifted to his. "How do we tell Christy's family that their daughter died because of two people's greed?"

He drew her close without answering, and Eve laid her head against his chest. "You're not alone," he whispered. "You have me, your father, and your mother. Jane and Betsy. We'll get through this together."

She tilted her head up to him. "I still have you? After the way I treated you back then?"

He framed her face. "Always. You'll always have me." He tipped her head back.

Tears glistened in her eyes. "I don't deserve you" she said. The words came out on a sob.

Her eyes told him everything he needed to know. He lowered his head and kissed her with all his heart. He had her back. He had the woman he loved back.

When the kiss ended, she nestled against him, and he was content to have her close.

"We have to do something to find that poor woman," Eve said. "She may have taken my place."

"We'll find her. I'm certain we will find her alive, and I plan on being part of the investigation. I owe it to the ones who died before her, and I owe it to you."

No matter how much it cost him, he would keep Eve safe. She'd been through enough.

Luke stepped from the station and spotted them.

"Are they being transferred to jail?" Trent asked, his voice unsteady.

"They are," Luke said. "And I have more news. Dispatch just received a call. We may have a lead on the Stalker case."

Trent's full attention was on Luke. "You do?"

"Someone called in after we broadcasted the description of the car we believe the Roadside Stalker is using," Luke said. "She spotted it driving around her place and my team is heading over there now."

"I'm coming with you," Trent told him, before facing Eve. "Go back inside with your father and stay here at the station where you'll be safe."

She grabbed his arm. "Trent."

The worry in her eyes made his heart soar. "I'll be careful. I promise." *I'm not going to miss my second chance with you.*

Once they were in Luke's SUV and following a line of police vehicles, Luke didn't waste time interrogating Trent.

"That seemed like more than a friendly interaction I interrupted."

He glanced at Trent. "You two getting back together?"

"I sure hope so," Trent replied.

"Looks like something good is going to happen from all of this after all."

"Where is this place we're headed?"

"The Blevins place," Luke answered. "We used to go fishing there when we were young, remember?"

Trent did. Mr. and Mrs. Blevins were both nice folks. Mr. Blevins passed away a few years back.

"There's something else," Luke continued, and Trent shifted in his seat.

The set of Luke's jaw told him it wasn't going to be good. He waited.

"You remember Douglas Blevins?"

"Of course. The Blevinses' grandson. We went to school with him. He left town after he graduated."

"Yeah, well, Mrs. Blevins thinks the car belongs to her grandson. She said the description sounded like the one he owns."

A terrifying sensation pressed down on Trent. "But he hasn't been back here in years, has he?"

"Not that I knew of."

Trent tried to remember the things he'd known about Douglas. He'd always been intelligent and a little geeky. He'd been the class valedictorian, had a full scholarship to an Ivy League school. The last Trent heard, he'd become a property law attorney and joined a big firm in New York. There was no way Douglas was a serial killer—was there?

They approached the Blevins property with caution. Several police cruisers pulled off the road ahead of them.

Trent got out, along with Luke, and went over to the line of officers piling out of patrol cars.

Luke updated each on the details they knew. He showed them a recent photo of Douglas.

Trent still couldn't accept that a guy who used to hang out with him occasionally might be a murderer. He remembered Eve telling him that Douglas had asked her outright if she and Trent were getting serious. Had Douglas harbored secret feelings for Eve? Was that the reason he had come after her?

"We believe Blevins is armed, dangerous, and holding a young woman hostage." Luke showed around the photo of Faith Harper.

Trent studied the young woman. She appeared to be in her twenties and bore a strong resemblance to Eve.

The hair on the back of his neck stood at attention. He didn't like the coincidence.

"If you're ready, we should go," Luke told him. "You're with me, and you don't go in first. Understood? You're not a detective anymore. If I get you hurt, it could be bad."

Trent agreed, and they headed to the area where Mrs. Blevins had seen the parked car on her property. There was an old abandoned trailer that had belonged to Douglas's parents before they died.

As the team neared the trailer, Luke suddenly stopped and pointed. A small sedan was parked behind the building, almost out of sight.

They advanced on the structure with precision. Someone inside immediately began shooting at them. The law enforcement officers ducked for cover. Trent and Luke hid behind some nearby trees. When the shooting stopped, they breached the trailer. Luke forced the door open.

In the living room, Douglas held the terrified young woman hostage, a knife against her throat. "I'll kill her if you come any closer."

Luke eased forward. "You don't want to do that, Douglas. Let her go. No one has to get hurt. We can help you."

Douglas waved the knife around. "How can you help me? I killed all those women."

Trent's gut twisted. Douglas had admitted to being the Roadside Stalker.

The murderer's wild eyes searched the sea of police around him and landed on Trent. "This is your fault."

Trent flinched. "You were in love with Eve, weren't you?" he asked gently. If he could keep Douglas distracted and talking, perhaps one of the officers would sneak up behind him and get his knife away to save the young woman.

"Eve was mine!" Douglas yelled. "She asked me to the autumn dance when we were juniors because she was interested in *me*—not you. We danced, and she told me how important I was to her. She was mine until you came along and turned her head. It was supposed to be me she chose, not you."

Trent remembered the time well. He hadn't been able to attend the dance, and Douglas didn't have a date. Eve had felt sorry for Douglas and told Trent she would take Douglas to the dance as a friend. She had never led him on, but Douglas had read too much into her kind offer.

"Is that why you started killing? You wanted to show Eve what you were capable of?" Trent kept his attention on Douglas's angry face while the officers behind the killer eased closer. "If you knew Eve at all, you'd know that's not the way to impress her. Especially since you targeted her."

"She was supposed to be with me—not you!" Douglas spat out again. "I had to make her pay for deserting me."

The officers were almost on top of the man.

"But you stopped killing for a while. You left me that note in my office to keep me from digging into the case." Trent had to keep him talking. "How did you know Eve was back in town?"

"I wanted to stop killing." Douglas moved the knife closer to Faith's throat. "I did, until I saw Eve getting gas in town and it all came flooding back. I could make her my crowning achievement before I stopped killing. So I followed her and got started. Except *you* showed up and interrupted. As usual."

"And you tried to get to her the following day, but I came along."

"You ruined everything!" Douglas shouted.

Faith spotted the officers closing in and tried to break free. Douglas released her and whirled. The officer closest tackled Douglas and disarmed him while the second pulled Faith out of harm's way.

Half a dozen officers descended. It didn't take long before Douglas, the Roadside Stalker, was subdued in handcuffs, still ranting at the top of his voice that all of it was Trent's fault.

Douglas's rights were read and he was led away, while EMTs escorted the young woman out to their vehicle to examine her.

Trent stared around the crumbling trailer. "I can't believe he's blamed me all these years. Imagined a relationship with Eve that didn't exist." Trent and Eve had been friends since they were children, though Douglas had always been on the outskirts of their group. While Eve treated everyone with importance, she and Douglas had never been more than friendly acquaintances.

"He's not stable." Luke stood beside Trent and watched as the CSI team descended on the scene and began gathering evidence. "I really hate that I have to tell Douglas's grandmother that he's the one who has been terrorizing the county."

Trent wondered if Mrs. Blevins may have suspected that something was wrong with her grandson. After all, she'd reported his car. Had Douglas been sneaking back to the area periodically to hunt for his victims?

Luke called him back to the present by saying, "Anyway, let's leave this to the crime scene techs and speak to Mrs. Blevins."

Trent shook his head sadly. "I knew both Mrs. Blevins and her husband. They used to let me help out around the farm for extra money." Even back then, Douglas had kept to himself, isolated in his room. He hadn't helped much around the farm. "What a mess. And I think we can assume Jacob and Samuel were using Blake's car to cast doubt on him. That would explain the adjusted driver's seat."

"Exactly," Luke said as they reached the SUV.

"Have you found the accountant yet?" Trent asked.

Luke glanced his way. "He was difficult to track down but, yes, finally. Apparently, Mr. Jenkins had a family emergency and had to be out of town for over a month, but he's on his way home. We'll get his statement as soon as he arrives." He drove the short distance to the main house.

Mrs. Blevins met them at the door. "Was that my Douglas? Is he okay?"

Luke asked if they could come inside and the older woman agreed. In the living room, Luke told her about the charges being brought against Douglas, and she put her head in her hands.

"I can't believe it—no. I hate to say it, but I can. There was always something off about my grandson."

"Like what?" Trent asked gently.

"Well, he had a cruel side to him. My husband noticed the way he tried to treat the farm animals and made him stay away from them. After his parents died, his behavior grew worse. He'd hole up in his room for hours on end. Then I'd wake up in the middle of the night and hear him walking around the house. He scared me, so I kept our bedroom door locked."

"Did you try to talk to him or get him some help?" Luke asked.

Trent could see how devastating it was to speak about, but Mrs. Blevins continued. "Many times. He simply became more closed off, resisted any kind of help we tried to get him. But when he went away to school, he seemed to get better. For a while." She looked between the two men. "He'd come home from time to time, and we would actually have a decent visit. I thought whatever was bothering him had passed." Tears filled her eyes. "He really killed those women?"

"We think so," Luke told her. "I'll need you to give an account of the times Douglas visited you when you're ready. We think they'll match up with the murders."

She straightened, lifting her chin. "Do you want me to come with you now? I'd like to see my grandson if I may."

"Of course."

Luke and Trent helped the elderly woman to the SUV.

The entire drive back to the station, Trent reeled. He couldn't imagine what Eve's reaction would be. Once they reached the station, Trent left Luke to deal with Douglas while he went to find Eve.

He opened the door to the conference room where the Lourdes family had gathered.

When Eve saw him, she jumped to her feet and raced to his side. "What happened? Are you all right?"

Trent did his best to explain Douglas's arrest without mentioning the man's obsession with Eve. It would all come out in time, but for now, she'd been through enough.

"Oh, Douglas, no," she said sadly.

"It will be a while before everything is sorted out." He glanced around the room at the weary faces. "You should all try and get some rest. My place isn't far from here. You're all welcome to stay there for as long as you want."

Jane rose and squared her shoulders. "That's very generous of you, Trent, but I wonder if you would be willing to take us back to the estate."

Trent understood the strength and determination behind the older woman's request. "Of course, but are you sure you want to see it now? Maybe you should wait until we've had a chance to clean it up."

Jane squared her shoulders. "I want to go now." She faced Eve. "I've changed my mind. I don't want to sell. I can't. After everything we've been through, I don't want to walk away from our family's heritage. We'll rebuild and make it better than before." She took Betsy's hand. "And I want you to be part of it. You are family, Betsy, and you always will be."

Betsy had tears in her eyes. "I would love that."

Melanie Cameron stepped into the room.

"Mom!" Eve ran to her mother and hugged her fiercely. "I'm so happy you're here."

Once Melanie had greeted her family, she faced Henry.

"I'll drive your mother back to the house," Henry assured Eve. "We have things to discuss."

Everyone stepped from the room to give them space.

With her seated beside him in the SUV on the way back to the estate, Trent wondered whether Eve would stay and help rebuild the family along with the home. Or would she leave him again?

When they arrived at the Lourdeses' property, the roads were still wet and muddy but no longer impassable. The fire department was still on-site, making sure it didn't reignite. In the light of day, it looked far worse. Most of the house was gone, with gaping holes where walls had once stood. The roof had collapsed, and nothing inside would be salvageable.

Eve clapped her hand over her mouth as she stared at her family home—another victim of Jacob and Samuel.

Trent pulled the vehicle up as close as he could to the rubble. Jane and Betsy got out, leaving the two of them alone.

"Are you okay?" Trent asked softly.

She turned to him, and to his surprise, she smiled. "It's just a house. Everyone is safe. The secrets that haunted me have been revealed. I'm free, Trent. Finally free. Soon, all the bad memories will fade, and then it will be time to make some wonderful new ones."

He clasped her hand in his, amazed by her strength. "With your parents' help and yours, Lourdes Mansion can be rebuilt."

She nodded. "They have a long road ahead, but Mom and Dad still love each other. Grandmother Jane has her family back, and she has the will giving her the rights to the estate."

Trent nodded. "And you are a business owner now. I have a feeling Jacob and Samuel left it in a financial mess. It will take a lot of work to get it back in order."

"I will do my best to keep Grandpa Alfred's legacy alive, no matter what that might involve." She sighed deeply. "Renee and Blake won't be happy to have us back."

"Maybe you can work through that and all become a family again, even stronger than before." He took a deep breath and forced himself to ask what he needed to know. "So, you're staying? You'll rebuild the house and fix the problems Jacob and Samuel left in the businesses?" *And finally come back to me*, he wanted to add, but didn't.

She searched his face. "I want to stay, Trent, but that depends on you. I love you. I realize I messed things up between us once. Can you ever forgive me? Because if not, I can't stay here and be reminded of—"

"I already have," he said gently. "I love you too, Eve Cameron. Will you stay and marry me?"

Tears filled her eyes. "You want to marry me? After everything I did?"

He gathered her close. "I've always wanted you to be my wife. Marry me, Eve."

"Yes! It will always be yes, Trent. Always."

She sealed the declaration of her love with a kiss.

He had her back. Nothing they'd gone through to get to this point mattered anymore. He had her back, and nothing would tear them apart ever again.

> *YOUR FEEDBACK MEANS A LOT TO US!*

Up to this point, we've been doing all the writing. Now it's *your* turn!

Tell us what you think about this book, the characters, the plot, or anything else you'd like to share with us about this series. We can't wait to hear from *you!*

Log on to give us your feedback at:
https://www.surveymonkey.com/r/InPeril

Annie's FICTION